From
The
34 Great Sut

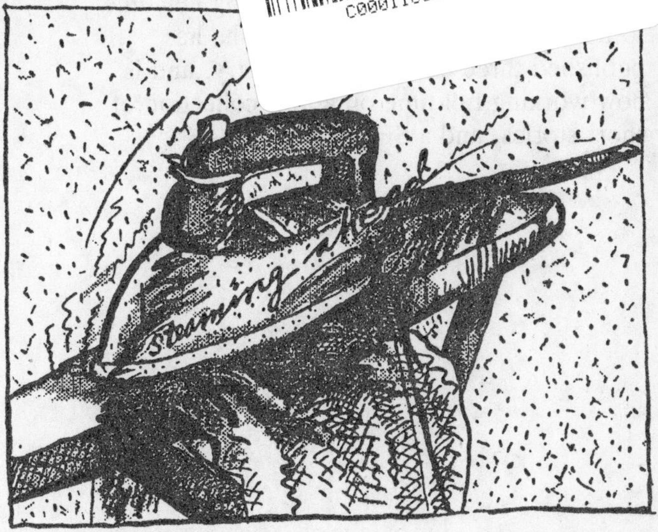

Candas Jane Dorsey was born in Edmonton, Alberta, and has lived most of her life there. She has worked as a social worker and as a teacher, although primarily devoting her time to freelance writing and editing. She has published three collections of poetry, and is now working full-time on a new collection of short stories, and a SF novel.

CANDAS JANE DORSEY

Machine Sex

and Other Stories

The Women's Press

First published in Great Britain by
The Women's Press Ltd 1990
A member of the Namara Group
34 Great Sutton Street, London EC1V 0DX

The following stories have been published previously:
'Johnny Appleseed on the New World' in *Tesseracts*, ed
Judith Merril, Porcépic Books, 1985; 'Black Dog' in *blue
buffalo*, 1984; 'You'll Remember Mercury' in *NewWest
Review*, 1980; 'Columbus Hits the Shoreline Rag' in
Getting Here, ed Rudy Weibe, NeWest Publishers, 1977;
'the white city' in *Dinosaur Review*, 1985; 'Willows' in
Tesseracts[2], ed Phyllis Gotlieb and Douglas Barbour,
Porcépic Books, 1987.

British Library Cataloguing in Publication Data
Dorsey, Candas Jane
  Machine sex . . . and other stories.
  I. Title
  813.54 [F]

ISBN 0–7043–4242–1

Typeset in 10½pt Times by Input Typesetting Ltd, London

Printed and bound by BPCC Hazell Books,
Aylesbury, Bucks, England, Member of BPCC Ltd

To my parents, Marie and Jack Dorsey,
my sister Jaclyn and brother Michael,
with love and thanks

Thanks also to past allies:
Cynthia, my familiar;
Whizaroo, the blind dog;
and Peter, for the footnotes

CONTENTS

CONTENTS

Sleeping in a Box

'Everything that is worthy is secret.'
Iris Murdoch

A school project to measure the size of the moon. What equipment will be necessary? The principal in his office has Rex Begonias in bloom; he rotates them from his greenhouse at home, bringing them through the cold corridors muffled in a quilt. He listens to the project idea expansively, but instead of granting permission begins to tell me about the cooking demonstration he gave earlier in the day. I haven't eaten yet today and his description is tangible in my mouth.

I have brought my blind dog in order to illustrate how I will explain graphically to the children the impossibility of measuring something without the right tools. A fine scientific principle. It is a long time since she last left the apartment and she is excited by the smell of children. She gyrates on the end of the leash almost as she did when she was young, dancing to the changing wafting odours she detects as currents in a stream. I could demonstrate with her a different measurement, one I cannot make; children's passage through this space is obvious to her, even though there are none here now and she couldn't see them anyway.

My apartment is down the hall from the large theatre in which the visitor from Earth performed. She sang well, but she wouldn't talk with us, and she gave us no encore though we applauded ferociously.

After the performance a few of us stayed in our seats, chatting among ourselves, and by an accident of acoustics Danno and I could hear the voices from backstage. Her manager was berating her for not talking between songs, for not responding to the applause.

She replied but what she said was not quite decipherable, spoken as it was in that charming accent.

Afterward I was in the corridor, fumbling for the key to unlock my apartment, when she came out of the theatre, alone and looking rather forlorn.

'Would you like to come for tea?' I asked.

She wanted to know how far it was; she had to be back at the hotel before a certain time.

'I live here,' I said, ducking under a painter's scaffold and opening the door. We were only a few metres from the theatre access door; she was amazed.

Inside, the apartment is charming: soft, easy furniture and big windows. The dog snuffled over to the singer, nosed her silk-clad knee. Her nose left a damp mark on the silk but the singer didn't notice, absorbed as she was in the view. I pretended to be blasé about the windows, though they had cost me a lot, and put on the kettle. Chara and Danno came over, we drank tea, the singer from Earth quiet, watching us, smiling formally whenever we looked at her. Her name was Meia.

On Earth it is not so difficult to know how big the moon is. My old lover once told me he could hold up his hand, thumb upwards, and at arm's length his thumb tip covered the moon. That's how big it is, where we all live, a disc no bigger than the thumb-nail of the average Terran. Under that nail we live jammed like so many grains of annoying sand, to be cleaned out now and again with a brush or the blade of a knife.

The singer from Earth stayed after the others left. I finally had to tell her I was going to make supper. Was she going to eat at the hotel? I asked.

'I have no plans,' she replied. 'May I eat with you?'

'I do not have enough,' I said.

'We can share,' she said. 'I don't eat much, really I eat like a bird.'

While I got out the plates and brought the food out of the cooler, she leaned against the counter. 'Can I help with anything?' she asked.

'No, it's fine,' I said. She reached a hand absently to pick up a piece I had just sliced. I put my hand over hers. 'Wait,' I said.

'Can I get out the rest?' she asked, her hand on the cooler door, opening it even as I said, 'That's all.'

The cupboard, of course, like the old rhyme, was bare. She wasn't stupid, she figured it out. 'That's all you have?'

'Until tomorrow. Yes. It's the end of the tenday. We have rations, we have to make them last.'

'But at the hotel, I get – '

'Yes. But you are from Earth. You have priority.'

'I will not eat after all. You will eat with me, at the hotel, as my guest.'

I wanted to go very much, but I know the Moon better than she ever will. 'They will not let you bring me in,' I said.

'I beg your pardon?'

'I will not be allowed. I will eat too much.'

'I will insist. I am their guest, after all.'

'You should reread your contract.'

She prepared to go. 'Wait,' I said. She stood looking at me, silk clothes so bright, in front of my very expensive windows. 'Never mind,' I said; 'goodbye.'

I said nothing more. Nevertheless, she seemed to think she should.

'I will come back,' she said after a silence. Then she went. I didn't expect to see her again.

I don't know if her visit had anything to do with it, but it was the morning after when I got the idea for the school project. I was down in the library, doing a little research, and I met the man who had been my first lover. I hadn't seen him in years. He had brought a delivery up from Earth. He was so pleased to see me that he stayed for some time with me, kissing and hugging me and talking about his children, who are teenagers now. 'Leaving you and deciding to have children were the best decisions I ever made,' he said effusively, between kisses. Then he went away to arrange for the return trip.

The library has an ice-cold water fountain. I drank a cup and refilled it. On Earth you can drink as much water as you like, leaving the tap running between cupfuls. It's one of the reasons I like the library.

Explaining my idea to the principal, I talk with my hands a lot, illustrating the relationships with the concept. The dog is restless and wants to get at the children. I don't mean to make it sound ominous. She just wants to play.

How big is the moon? How big are any of us? When I am as hungry as I am now I feel thin but not very small. Though I am as narrow as a thread, my hunger makes me enormous.

The windows look so real. Cars, aeroplanes, pedestrians walking in and out of frame, out there on Earth, as if they were outside my walls. The singer from Earth is fascinated.

Really, *from* Earth: she has now left Earth for this place, strange though I find that. She walks around my apartment, touching things. I don't like her to touch too much; she'll see what's fake. The blind dog is tracking her by sound, orienting herself by bumping the furniture. The dog is allowed to touch.

Meia is her name; I suppose I should try to remember that. She will want me to call her by her name. All the Earth people do. She will want me to ask her how she is settling in, and profess interest in her reactions to the move. She will want me to ask her what she finds most different, most similar, most challenging and welcoming. Well, if these conversations give me back enough, maybe I will take her to the library. She will like the water fountain, but only after she has been here long enough to appreciate it.

The library is not for newcomers. It is for people who have been sleeping in this particular box for a long time.

Night, according to the windows. Meia is here again. Talking at length for the first time, saying – do I want to know?

'I don't care so much about the size,' she says. 'It's the colour of it.' Is she talking about the food, her room, or her lover? I forget. She notices me forgetting.

'Why do you do that?' she suddenly says.

'What?'

'That . . . removal. That deafness. All you people here do it. You ask me questions and then you don't hear the answers and half the time you ask me the same questions again the next day. Why ask me the questions if you don't want to know? Heaven knows it's hard enough to figure out what you want me to answer. I'd be just as happy not to say a thing.'

'But then you'd touch things.'

I didn't mean to say that, it just came out.

'Touch things?'

I turn away but I can't get away from the conversation to which I committed myself. 'You touch our things. They're ours. Some of them came from Earth. They were expensive. They belong to us, not you. If you want something, get it yourself. Don't use up ours.'

'You mean, there's a rule about it? Nobody told me.'

'We don't tell people from Earth. They'd get uncomfortable and we can't stand that. But if you move here, someone finally tells you things. I'm sorry it had to be me.'

'Why? You are my friend. I'd rather you tell me than some stranger.'

'No, I'm not your friend. I told you, we don't touch other people's.'

'Other people's what?'

'Everything. Other people's everything.'

'Welcome to the moon,' she says.

'It's called the box,' I say. 'The moon isn't this place, and this place isn't the moon. Look,' and I gesture out my windows.

'It's not Earth either,' she says. 'Those windows are transmitted from down home just like everything else.'

'Oh, yes,' I say, 'but they cease to be Earth soon enough. Do you know how to measure the size of the moon?'

'No,' she says.

'Start by touching it,' I say. 'That's the answer. And we never will. So the moon's as big as we imagine it to be.'

'Which is how big?'

'Well, today, it doesn't exist at all,' I tell her. 'She can tell you,' and I indicated the blind dog, who all this time had been fawning at either Meia's knee or mine.

'She's allowed to touch things,' Meia says, sharper than I gave her credit for being.

'Yes, but she can't see,' I say with sorrow.

'Is that my option too? To touch and be blind, or to see and be alone? Or to get myself a deaf cat, or a lame bird, or another dog like this? Or some of these phony windows?'

'No,' I say. 'It's not like that. The dog is old; I'm used to her now. I have friends, lovers, we have our lives. We know what's what, so we don't have to dissemble with each other. We know where the windows come from, but we know where they go, too. That's the difference.'

'And I can't be one of you and know too?'

'You will be, whether you like it or not. Unless your singing is so fine that they ask for you back.'

'I didn't exactly have a choice about leaving – only a choice of exiles. When I played here, it seemed fine. Now I see where the punishment lies.'

'We are all bitter. Maybe not about the same things.'

I go up to her and put my fingers through her hair to her warm scalp. I can feel her firm skull holding my hands apart.

'I like my head held,' I say. 'Do you? I think I live there, inside my head. If you ever want to touch me, really reach me, touch me like this.' And I stroke her ears, her brow, through her hair, and her strong neck. She looks at me with a surprised, then a troubled, finally a rebellious face.

'Why are you doing this?' she whispers.

'To make you understand,' I say. 'Besides, I have always liked your singing.'

She pulls her head away roughly, pushes the dog's head away from her lap, gets up and half-rushes, half-stumbles to the door.

I want to keep a proper silence, to teach her, but suddenly: 'Do you see why I didn't want it to be me?' I had to ask her.

'No,' she says, 'but I am sure I will sometime understand. When I have been well and thoroughly boxed-in to this place.' And she goes out, as I intended her to do.

For the first time, I miss her a little, later.

In the library, there are workers around the ice water fountain. They are putting in a wall. I walk to the fountain. One of the workers is Danno.

'This is the last day,' he says. 'As of next tenday, it's to be restricted. Card holders only.'

'That's not right,' I say. 'This is the library!'

But there is nothing to be done. I go home to my apartment, where the blind dog waits.

Project to measure the size of the moon. How long is a piece of string? The schoolchildren will learn more than triangulation, but I don't tell the principal about that. I have my own ideas about how big the Moon has become. I have spent a lot of time walking through these halls, and living in that apartment with its clever windows. This morning when I woke up, it was because I had tried to stretch in my sleep, rolled over in bed, and struck my shoulder and arm right down to the knuckles against the wall that bounds the bed. The pain abolished sleep. I have been here a long time but my body will not always forget.

Johnny Appleseed on the New World

         I think the winds terrify me. There is no logic in the sand. There is no reason in the shifting world that covers up everything we have done. Slowly all that we have built is becoming nothing. Slowly the tendrils of sand erase it. The others are angry. My imagination sees a power behind it; my reason says no god abhors us. The result is only fury, a simple emotion hanging like a knot, like a stone, in the centre of my body.

Lesje, the partner with whom I share a shelter, is concerned. She doesn't know whether I am sick or crazy or both. The new world is alien. It has done something to every one of us. She can't figure out what it has done to me. She goes out every morning grumbling, comes back apprehensive, wondering if I've done something stupid.

I have chosen, instead of my regular work, to mend the membranes when they wear thin. She thinks maybe I will neglect this job? She thinks I want the sand in my mouth, while I sleep?

The pod is small, only seven of us living here. The walls

were once transparent so we lived among the land, separated only by a membrane. Now the skin is scoured to opacity, so that all we see of outside is dark and light and, when the sand blows, vague shadows shifting above, around. Thin patches on the membrane show shiny and grainy as silk. I go around with a container of membrane material, smoothing it onto the thin bits with a brush, like an ancient House Painter. The brush is made of our hair, recycled. We had to do something with it.

In the old stories we would go crazy, the seven of us cooped up in this planetbound space capsule. Or else we would have been chosen by psychological screening and a bad apple would have got in by accident.

I think I would like to taste an apple. We are supposed to grow them here, the trees were begun on the journey, from the cryonically preserved seeds or cells or some such. That was Heather's business. On the journey, and when we were first here, she was the laughing outward one of us.

Now she stays in her research area a great deal, trying to keep the hydroponics healthy without enough natural light. Of course, they were all designed for this sun, and the shade of the scrubbed dome is too much shade, and our lamps are solthree wavelengths.

Lesje worries because I am not able to do my work.

She worries because I have decided to patch the tent instead. She thinks I don't get enough exercise.

Outside the tent the wind is blowing.

I remember when we first came here, there was a brilliant light on the silver sand beaches, something like the light of Greece. (On Earth now, Greece is part of the History Preserves, to ensure that nothing will further erode the ancient broken marble. Even the gentle wind wore away too much; the energon coating was being put on the Parthenon as we flew away.)

We all remember the journey differently, but it isn't the journey that is important. All the decisions had been made on Earth, and all the action would be made on the new world, so we amused ourselves, on holiday from the universe.

We came here in the spring, when the light was white and bright and cool. We had the long summer to build, the long autumn to rest. Now it is winter.

And the wind blows all the time.

Well, never mind. That's my mantra: oh well, never mind, I repeat to myself. It helps. I find a place in the membrane where the striations are so deep, so close to our side of the tent, that I can see the landscape again. The sand has drifted around the space-grown, firm-planted fruit trees, and among the trees the outside workers ('the husbands' we call them jokingly) are walking ponderously in their membrane suits, only their heads showing through because we replace the helmets regularly. The bodies of the suits are opaque like the tent, and for the same reason.

I crouch there, looking out the tiny peep-hole, for a long time. Finally I paint on the coating of membrane. The air is not so warm these days, so the patch takes longer to harden. The thickness distorts the image through the tiny strip of light, removes the camera effect. To get back the transparent quality, I would have to paint the other side as well, smooth it off.

I think it is time for an uprising, a change.

We have divided the work along lines of capability. Four go out to tend the garden. Heather, Sam and I work inside. The three of us do housework.

I agreed to the division at the time, even chose the factions and gave the teams their foolish names. Though we are only seven, it was a useful way to order the winter's activities.

Now I think it is time we wives got out of the kitchen, so to speak. That smug metaphor keeps me chuckling until the husbands come home. Mine, that is, Lesje, looks at me as if I'm strange.

Well, I am. We all are. The secret of compatibility on a long space voyage and subsequent settlement, I propound to myself (painting the dome and making the most of every

stray idea), is to put a randomly chosen assortment of toler-
ant weirdos and expert improvisers into a membrane shell
and accelerate them off to the stars. It isn't necessary even
to hope for the best. Whatever happens, happens. After a
while the planners drop in, riding a more conventional craft
with a conventional crew chosen carefully for their stability
and thus with the usual assortment of crazies and a psychotic
locked up in the brig since maybe Arcturus when s/he broke
a few important things and some heads, and marvel at their
intelligent choice of pioneers, wishing only that the upstart
offspring swarming around would show more of the proper
respect and attitude. (Unfortunately, their parents have
taught them that the idiots who sent them off to live in a
membrane and plant apple trees, like some kiddie mytho-
logical figure, on an unsuitable planet are just that, idiots,
and don't even deserve the free lunch they're being served,
but it's in the contract.)

So. We have got this far in the scenario; we have arrived.

There are no offspring yet. We haven't had a chance to
unfreeze any seed. Just apple trees, drifting over with sand.

These are the thoughts with which I occupy myself as I
pull my brush back and forth, meditating on beginnings and
voyages and solutions, finally thinking only of the slow and
rewarding stroke of the membrane material, smooth under
the spreading bristles of hair.

I turn suddenly and there is a figure behind me. One of
the others? No. Long robe with hood, long face within the
hood. Dimly seen, maybe young, hard to tell, the face is
shadowed. Smiling, not menacing, but still, a stranger.

On a world where there are no strangers.

I have decided to go back to my own job. I start with
Heather in her hydroponics lab.

'Don't you feel like getting outside?' I say.

'How do you like these low-light hybrids?' she counters.
'I'm breeding them with tough bark, like the apple trees,
and maybe I can get them out next winter.'

'How long is it until spring?' says Samuel, coming in with

her carving tool in one hand, a carefully-worked piece of apple wood in the other.

She shows it to us. Heather nods approvingly, familiarly. I take the carving in my hands. It is a tender and meticulous rendition of a hooded person, face smooth and smiling, folds of robe carefully carved. She has been polishing it until it has a patina.

'I see another gardener most days now,' says Heather quietly.

'Am I the last one to twig to this?' I ask. I pick up a branch of one of the hybrids; a thorn scrapes my finger. Irritated, I say, 'What in the world are they doing out there, anyway?'

Heather grins. I peel a piece of membrane material off my finger. Under it the skin is clean and healthy; the scratch stops where the membrane material began.

At dinner Lesje is irritable. 'They're not going to last until spring,' she says snappishly to Heather. 'Look at this.' The apple branch is scoured clean of bark on one side only, polished to almost a shine. The broken end is rough. The gnarls of the grain look like the folds of a robe. Heather shrugs, shakes her head.

'Another suit filter went today,' says Anna. 'No spares until the supply ship comes in the spring.'

'Tanj,' swears Lesje furiously.

'I was right,' I say.

'They've held up this long,' says Jed. 'The winter's just been longer and tougher than we expected.'

'What, the trees or the filters?' asks Lesje.

'Either.'

'Pfui.'

Nihio says, 'The settlers who took over my part of the world in ancient history used to get crazy in the winter. Too much of the same thing. Bushed, they called it.'

I don't mention the figure to the husbands. No one is talking. Sam has put her carving into my hand. 'I thought I was getting a taste of that kind of crazy, at first,' she says.

I was the last of us to see it. I wonder what Lesje and Jed, Nihio and Anna see, outside all day.

'Tomorrow I think we should take over the outside detail,' I say, and the discussion about that lasts until midnight. Finally the decision is made, though Lesje is reluctant.

'You don't know that orchard like we do,' she says.

'All the better,' says Jed, and Lesje casts him an angry look, but in the end agrees to trade jobs with Heather.

In the morning, the husbands crowd around us as we put on the three worn suits with the clear helmets. I have taken a container of energon and one of the recycled-hair brushes. Heather has a few of her new plants. Samuel has her wood-collecting bag. She used to send it out with Nihio, so he could get driftwood for her. Windfalls.

As our four figures go into the airlock, Heather holds back the door until the fourth one's robe has cleared the door-track. She makes sure her hands don't touch the soft folds. We don't look for a reaction in the four we leave inside. None of us really wants to know yet.

The first day I paint three trees with energon on the windward side. Some sand is trapped in the coating as it dries, but that shouldn't matter. Looking back at the dome I see suddenly why the whole tent surface is scoured. The membrane is, accidentally, a perfect airfoil shape, wide end into the wind, so that the sand is drawn across the whole surface before blowing away behind. I flew sailplanes above the Parthenon; I remember drifting supported by that white, hot light.

The second day Lesje and Nihio agree to turn the tent against the wind. I paint four trees with membrane material, to test whether a more flexible coat will let them grow better.

The third day, I paint the downwind side of the tent from the outside while Lesje paints the inside. As our strokes cross, we become clear to each other, she with her face set and unsmiling, wielding the brush like a windstorm.

The fourth day, Lesje puts on the defective suit, comes out at midday and shovels the drifted sand away from the new window. She and Jed have moved the hydroponics to the window area. I have stopped sleeping in the shelter with her and that night I put my pallet under the leaves near the window side of the tent. In the night, I wake to see the figure sitting nearby, hood back, looking out into the orchard. When I move, the calm face looks over at me, a hand raises slightly. I turn over and sleep again.

After a few days' activity outside, Lesje is coughing intermittently, but to Jed's concern she snaps, 'Never mind, I'm fine. No one ever got black lung disease and died in this short a time. The Bedouins lived in this stuff all their lives, and they didn't have all this fancy technology.'

'Well, put your robes across your noses tomorrow and come out,' says Heather, 'because I think the trees are budding.'

'When winter comes can spring be far behind?' says Anna, then laughs his hearty laugh.

Lesje even smiles.

The blossoms are battered by a few spring storms, but gradually the sand slows and stops and we can shovel the drifts away for good, and paint the tent clear. We leave the airlock open as we do it, though the air is cooler than complete comfort, and run in and out with our paintbrushes, making our winter womb into a window again.

'Okay, Yanni,' Lesje says to me one day, her hand caressing a branch, 'okay. But I wish I'd thought of it.'

The blossoms scent the air for a while, then fall away. The eight of us work among the trees, clearing the last of the sane dunes, checking the results of the energon and the membrane tests, finding the membrane worn and cracked but the trees healthier than the three energon-protected ones. I had only painted the upwind sides of any tree, so we can take a rigid and perfectly detailed tree-print in energon from the three test trees, leaving them to grow in health. I stand the energon casting in the middle of the tent, and call the triangle they encircle the art gallery. Samuel hangs her carvings on the transparent half-branches.

The fruit begins to ripen, turns from green to tentative red to a deep shine. We decide that when we find the first windfall, that day will be the beginning of the harvest.

The light is white and clear and brilliant as I walk out among the orchard and find, fallen in the thick grass that has grown across the sand beneath the trees, a ripe red apple. I pick it up and take a bite. The fruit is slightly pink, veined with red, and the taste is strange and intense. It is the first apple I have ever held in my hand like this, have ever touched or tasted. To stand under our own trees with the breeze in my face and bite deeply into the fruit of our long year's work – I came a long way to this. I hand the rest of the apple to my companion, who is walking with the hood of the robe pushed back so the wind gently lifts the thin strands of dark hair.

The long brown fingers grasp the alien fruit and the hand takes it slowly to a smiling mouth. Our new companion takes a bite, chews and swallows.

'It's sweet,' I say.

The smile is sweet that answers me.

Death and Morning

He crossed the great bridge singing. It was Mid-summer Night Eve and he was bound for a party in the town, he was dressed in his best. Diana is my darling, he was singing. And so she was to be.

This was a high-tech planet, my children. He had smoothed the hair from his face with a machine, he wore clothes of synthetic thread, he was a bright young blade cutting his high-tech way through the night. On his side of the bridge the streets were dark, but as he crossed, the lights came on all over town. He hurried on, his rather pale skin glowing now, with anticipation and romance.

She shone in his thoughts like airport lights, she was the runway to which he aimed. He sang as he banked and turned, adjusted his trim, flew through the night toward her. Automatic direction-finders corrected his course; he was thinking of the flight to come.

The troopers were out that night, the thought police, but he never checked his pace, though he checked their positions for further reference. They could not darken him, he was on the right side of the bridge, and he was alight. On the corner of the centre square, she met him.

She was a child of a good family, gone to crime for kicks, who had Baader-Meinhoffed her way through the finishing school of two or three other planets before coming home to cool out, go straight, play it for keeps.

Now she was just a teenaged bombshell and she made the most of what she had.

'My darling,' he said.

'Ah,' she said.

'I am on fire for you,' he said, and she saw it was true.

'Do you love me?' she asked.

'With all my convictions,' he replied.

She took him into her arms, she took him in to her arms.

'I will show you how to use this for my pleasure,' she said. He took up the machine in his hand, for they were on a high-tech planet, and the touch of it was electric.

'Anything. Everything,' he said.

She taught him range, and direction, and duration. They went into the gallery, and she taught him from a distance and at close quarters. There was the dance of approach, the touch of contact, the leap of conquest, the silent withdrawal. There was fire, and there was ice.

'Ah, you are good,' she told him. 'Better than most that they send me from the other side.'

'I am a volunteer,' he said.

In the night he danced, spun and turned, flipped and glided. The fire of his passion, yes, that is what it was, my children, the fire was fierce within him.

'Ah, freedom,' he cried. 'Ah, my heart.'

Over and over she put him through the motions, over and over she corrected him to better form. She was a voice and a hand and a shape in the night, she was a draught for his fire, to keep it blazing, she was fuel for it, to never let it fade or die.

'You will never die,' she said to him.

'Never die,' he murmured.

Yet there was a little death in every moment. There is always a little death.

Reflect, my children, on the nature of time. While Rip van Winkle bowled with the Little People one night, while the princess lived beneath the sea with the moon for a year, while Semley journeyed her brief journey to bring back the necklace, the rest of the world grew old. The wind blew, the rain fell, the sun rose and shone elsewhere, but all the time he was with her seemed but a long night, a single long night.

That is the way of things. It was the way of things in her house, in her chambers, in her heart. The years outside rolled by, but she was forever young, and he was young, with her. Learning and learning, and the long night passing, and time in it for all the passions to fill and swell, find voice and action, find purpose and meaning.

Sometime in the night:

'This is a spray-action, unidirectional gas. The immediate effect is disorientation and vertigo. You can use it safely as long as you don't walk through the spray. The dispersal rate is very slow and the substance breaks down quickly in most atmospheres, so by the time it spreads it is harmless. In those affected, there may be a secondary effect once they begin to wake, an effect of hallucination and formless violence. This need not concern you as long as you are not within arm's reach at the time.'

'Ah, freedom,' he repeats.

Or:

'What do you do when you meet the Prince?'

'Which time?'

'Let's say the first time, in the receiving line.'

'I say, your Majesty, I am thrilled. Your sybaritic fame precedes you.'

'No! Wrong! Again.'

'Your Majesty, your fame as a sybarite precedes you.'

'Good. Then?'

'Whatever the reply is, I say, I am available for your pleasure if you would so honour me tonight.'

'And if I am the Prince, and you meet me?'

'Your Majesty, your fame as a sybarite precedes you.'

'You are a lovely boy and I want to ravish you.'

'I am available for your . . . '

'No! You have already been asked! Use your imagination!'

'With delight, your Majesty.'

'That's better. Again.'

'Your Majesty, your fame as a sybarite precedes you.'

'You are a silly young man. I only make it with girls.'

'Your Majesty, I am a girl. Pray, I am available for your pleasure if you would so honour me tonight.'

'Not bad. But get rid of that hesitation there, and put more eagerness in. But your Majesty, I *am* a girl. . . '

And:

'The garrote is the oldest of weapons. We use it a great deal. It is quiet and quick and can't fail you in a power outage. No batteries to run down. If you run a warp of thin wires through your belt it will show up on the detectors merely as decorative weaving, and you will have three or four to use in series. The difficulty is handles, for the wire will slit your hands as easily as the neck of the enemy. Best to have them already attached, as part of a decorative buckle. This new poly fibre is the best – it's almost invisible. It's best to leave the fibre in the wound. Take the handles, of course, they can be traced, but leave the wire. Trying to retrieve it is unnecessarily messy. Now go and practise on the golems until you can do the over-and-twist in one motion.'

'Oh, my heart,' he said, killing a simulacrum which fought with realistic fervour. He was bruised from that one, but the next laid no hand on him, and the last never sensed him except at the moment of dying.

Then:

'And what do you do when you see the prince?'

'I go and undo the shirt. I run my hand over the breasts

and the belly, then as I caress the genitals with the other hand, I open the ring above the heart. Can't you find a less primitive way than a ring? And jewelry is not the fashion this year.'

'It will be.'

'I mean it. I feel better about the idea of an implant or a skin disc. You have that kind of thing, don't you?'

'Ah, my darling one, you are getting too sophisticated for us, with your beyond-the-bridge cleverness. Yes, we can do that, but there is more danger for you. If it touches your skin, you are gone too.'

'Then change my skin.'

So the night went on, and he was changed in it. Layer by layer he was peeled back to the bone, rebuilt by her, tender fingers over him, thrilled to the core, taken apart and then made one again. You think he was high-tech before! Afterward, oh, afterward, my children, he was far beyond that. But still, the fire, the fire, and she was his stoker. She heaped on the coals, higher and higher. He sang a fierce battle song. She smiled, young and lovely. She was his lighthouse, he sailed to her guidance.

This was what he had come for. This was what he had come to.

Now not to say there was no love in it, my children. There was love in all of it, as I have been telling you. When he came across from the dark side of town, he came for love, for love of her. She rewarded him for it with special lessons. In all his lessons he learned fast, but in these he was the best, for he had her sweet body as a reward as well as an encouragement. But these rewards began to seem only diversions and as they lay after coitus he would say, 'And if I have to kill him from the side, from inside his field of vision?'

And she would show him.

Then as he danced in his room alone, dancing the dance of death, practising the dance of death – 'Allow me, o

Prince, to touch your perfect body . . . ' – he heard the bell toll the first stroke of the hour, and she came to him.

'Midnight,' she cried, 'the witching hour! Up and away! To horse! The Red Death! Oh, come beloved, if you love me!'

In his best clothes, dressed for a party. Singing again as on the bridge. It seemed hardly a moment had passed since he met her in the street that is not called Straight. Out of his eyes burned the fever, the love of her, and of more than her, the love of death. For in love, there is always a little death, as I have told you.

Through the streets with her, where the troopers stood back, watching them, watching the untouchables alight with purpose, though their purpose seemed the purpose of Midsummer at midnight: to dance, to love, to sing. And a great slow ringing of the bell, the second stroke.

Through the streets to the golden door, and the golden door stood wide, and within, singing and laughter. At the door, a hollow-cheeked attendant, who took their cloaks, looked hungrily at the trays of food as they were carried past, but these were not for the common folk.

'Ah, my heart,' he cried, with what exhilaration and despair only she knew, and she smiled at him, teen bombshell primed and charged, and seeing in him her explosion.

'You are the best they have sent me,' she said.

'I am a volunteer,' he replied. The bell tolled.

'Come, meet the Prince,' said a silver-clad one, a silver lamé vision, high-heeled strapless, oh, very high-tech, and very very gracious.

'My delight,' he said, his smile wide, a song on his lips, and he crossed the long room amid the hum of machinery, sex and hate. He saw her face as it faded behind him, for a moment in the bright light becoming its true age, wrinkling and crumbling like paper that has been consumed in the fire. He turned his head back a fraction, the better to see her, but he thought, it was a trick of the light and shadow, for her bright vivacity was turned to the Prime Minister, saying, ' . . . of the third quarter, and I said to him, well, frankly, no, it's too low-tech. . . '

The bell.

Now the Prince was before him, greeting the silver one, who touched forehead to the royal hand, said, something, and the Prince turned to him, and said:

'What a beautiful young boy! Why; we haven't had a boy here in, how long, my dears?'

'Your Majesty, I am honoured, your fame as a sybarite precedes you.'

'As well it should. And what is your name?'

'Call me anything you like, Majesty. I am available for your pleasure if you would so honour me tonight.'

'And how long since we had such a well-spoken one? Well, let me see,' and the royal hand evaluates him, breast, buttock, thigh and groin. 'Yes, indeed I believe there's something there.'

And indeed there was, for he had been trained very well indeed. Seeing that, the Prince laughed and said, 'Take the boy to my suite after the feast. I'll want him alone.' He was dismissed into the dancing, and his heart was leaping with love. He swirled past her in the dance but she didn't see him through those wide staring eyes, burning eyes. Fever. He was on fire also, a dervish in the midnight.

Again the bell. Eating. Again the bell. Dancing. Again the great ringing. Again.

Then finally the one in lamé, the courtier, courier, came to take our loving lad to the Prince.

They went through corridors, down stairs. There were places where candle-light flickered, and stretches where fluorescent tubes gleamed with bare ferocity. The first stair was carpeted and hung with arras, the second was tiled and metal-edged, the third was carved wood with gold balustrades. He was humming quietly, smiling occasionally at the silver guide, who smiled back coolly, put a long thin hand on his back, on his thigh, between his legs as he went ahead up the stairs. Ah, freedom, he thought, and touched the hand; it was cold as hell is cold, he thought. Another ringing of the bell, and a corridor, and a great door, tooled in gold. The silver-clad one's hand reached to open it, and at the same time a voice from behind them:

'No! Wait!'

A trooper, running, blood running from his nose and ears, and from a gaping defense cut in his hand.

He heard snatches of the gasped explanation, the Prince already gone from the dining hall, gone from the dancing, Diana a firebrand, exploding bombshell, death of the Prime Minister, death and chaos. He killed the guard with a blow to the larynx, used his first garrote on the silver one, felt the thin strand sink into the soft throat, the arched body struggling, then still. There was a room to the side, where he could leave the bodies, he thought, and dragged them there to the sound again of the bell. A current had intensified in his body, his head was bursting with melody and joy. He tasted the blood of the trooper, knelt to put his lips against the hand and suck; he was curious about the silver one, what sex, what body, he put his hand to the lamé to tear it away, tore, but it was skin, a great loose shining skin folded across alien genitals, he thought of the Prince, rooting into that alien soil; he thought of the Prince, who had already left the dancing, and ran back to the golden door, pulled it open, went in.

Inside there was a conventional kind of luxury. Reflect, my children, on that hopeless result of a voracious desire for novelty. Our lad thought with love of his home in the darkness, thought of the unlimited potential of technology, thought of freedom. He was coming in for a landing, now, seeing her lights in his mind's eye. He stood amid the furs and silks, the satins and downs, the cedars and precious metals, the rarity of wood and natural fibres in this high-tech place pounding in his thoughts to the rhythm of his song. He licked the last of the blood from his mouth, he felt the power of his lust, he felt the moment of her death, he felt her as she escaped torture into death, he felt her fire

enter into his body to mount with his own, he heard the
bell, the penultimate stroke, he turned back to the door,
the Prince came in.

'Your Majesty.'

'Come here, sweet boy.'

Those royal lips on his, tasting the blood; the Prince drew
back, laughing, 'You have an exotic tipple, little one! We
will share a cup when we are done. I will have a commoner
killed. Who did you kill?'

'A trooper. I was hungry.'

'Delightful! And my cicisbeo?'

'Drank with me.'

'But you are still pure, I hope.'

'I have waited for this all my life, Majesty. I have saved
myself for you.'

'You won't regret that.'

'No, I won't.'

And he went to the Prince, and opened the silken shirt,
and ran his hand over the soft cold rounded breasts, over
the roll of belly. He brought his other hand to the genitals,
pulled aside the kirtle, found warmth and wet and hardness,
put his hand above the heart, opened the skin disc, felt the
convulsion in the body where it writhed on the point of his
fingers, felt the fire mount to a crescendo, burst through
every fibre of him, the climax of all his foreplay, took his
hands away and let the corpse crumble to the floor.

'Ah, Prince,' he said. 'I have killed you. Ah, Freedom.'

And the bell tolled the last stroke of the change, and was
silent. In the silence he heard the Empire falling.

Running, back along the corridor, the carved stairs, the
tiled back stairs, the arras-hung stairs. Through a ballroom
empty but for the dead, through the feasting hall strewn
with the poisoned meats, through the outer hall where the
cadaverous attendant crouched, tearing with its teeth, by a
trooper's body. Into the brilliant streets.

Running back to the darkness, laughing and singing and
feeling his flesh melting around him with the heat of the

fire, seeing his flesh melting, knowing that the psionic command that had loosed the Prince's poison had loosed his own destruction. Knowing that his entirely predictable false lover had rebuilt him for one job only, and the job was done. She had expected her own death, and ensured his, but the Prince was gone and the war had begun, and when the dawn came, it would be Midsummer Day.

All the trooper positions he had noted for his escape – they were all irrelevant now. He burned for her for the final loving time, for the final song, for the final moment, burned to a cinder and was consumed.

Then he saw a span before him, and darkness on the other side. For this is the way of it, my children; death is a bridge, a great bridge between one place and another.

And he crossed the great bridge, singing.

The Prairie Warriors

I

The first image is the prairie warrior, riding down
from the hills in the first frost of autumn, the hooves of her
graceful, tiny-footed mountain pony cutting into the grasses
made crisp by ice. Snick, snick. Snick.

She is dressed all in the tradition, in the chain-link vest
and with the sword beside her hip. In the mountains it is a
very traditional story. The sword swings an arc keeping
obscure time to the finicky steps of the horse, and it rings
on the point of the arc when the hilt hits the mail, so our
warrior is a little foreign symphony as she rides in from the
hills. She makes a sweet little singing too, until almost the
time she comes in sight of the village, but they do not hear
her for she remembers herself in time.

She is a special envoy, a particularly chosen emissary from
the prairies. In the prairies she is well-respected for her
skills. In the mountains she is feared. She rides like that.
She brings all the tiny threatening noises of the prairie with

her to terrify the mountain birds, though to do them credit they seem remarkably calm, singing away their little hearts without a care, ruffling their feathers and complaining that it is winter but oblivious to the prairie woman who rides among them, her bright blonde hair streaking and tangling in the wind.

None of them should ignore her. Too much depends on the mood of menace she brings with her.

The second image is of a frightened girl shivering half-dressed in a village square. The wind of morning from the heights brings the smell of ice from the upper glaciated valleys, but she is dressed, as custom demands, in only a cotton shift with no sleeves. She has crossed her arms and hugged them to her chest, not just to try to keep warm, but also to hide the scars that are cross-hatched up and down the soft skin of her forearms.

At her feet there is a bundle, and thrown across it a fur wrap. Beside her on the ground is a soft leather shirt with a cotton-lined yoke. The yoke is embroidered with a complex pattern, which doesn't show as the shirt is carefully, ceremoniously folded. Under the shirt in the stack of clothes is a pair of suede leather trousers, and a pair of boots with tall soft tops folded down like seven-league boots in a story book. They are the best clothes she has ever had. She has not yet been allowed to touch them.

She looks very tired, and all the shivering is not from cold either, as all the hugging was not. She is suffering more than anyone knows, and her body is in that chilled and feverish state where the senses are preternaturally sensitive. So she has been watching the prairie warrior for quite a long time before the others in the village turn their heads to the slick sound of crackling frozen grasses and the pony walks into the circle of hostile welcoming people.

The third image is of a middle-aged woman on the edge of the crowd. She is the only one who knows both the prairie warrior and the waiting girl, and the only one who knows what this exchange means. The people of the prairie have been coming here to take prisoners every seven or eight years (depending on the moons' cycles) since this woman can remember. It is the result of a treaty signed four generations ago by the defeated people of the mountains with the victorious prairie warriors; the treaty came after a long winter of hunger and involved ritual hostage exchanges and immediate and ongoing supplies of food, the first to come from the mountains to the prairie and the second to flow in the other direction. The mountain people have always felt ill-used in the trade but they eat well in winter now although they are no better at tilling their tiny valleys than they were fifty years before.

She is Maddega, and she embroidered the shirt.

II

When the drugs had taken me a long distance, I could reach back with a long hand and pick up something sharp, could cut my arms before anyone noticed, least of all myself. Dopa is supposed to be very tranquil stuff, so the people were always surprised, but Maddega stitched my wounds with her sterile needle and eventually when the pain arrived at me, or I returned to it, she would rock me until I stopped crying and started wanting her instead. She seldom wanted me then, but sometimes we made an arrangement. I was seventeen, after all, old enough to know what I needed.

'Foolish one,' was always her answer. 'You don't even know what you want.' But she taught me a great deal.

She was a retired warrior, though she didn't seem that old to me, old enough to have to stop fighting. When I told her so she laughed, which I thought was not fair, and said she put in for retraining and reassignment.

'Then what happened?' I asked, but she wouldn't say.

'Never mind,' she said, 'when the prairie people come for you you'll find out everything you want to know.'

'Everything?' I teased, and she grinned and said, 'Get on away, I have work to do. Go practise something.'

'What?'

'You are seventeen now; you know what you need,' she said, 'so you decide.'

And because the drug had receded enough, I could work, and I went riding, or climbing, or practising swordplay on the field, though I was no good at it and Maddega just laughed.

III

I had been a long time waiting for this implacable blonde warrior to carry me away. I had been dreaming of the prairie warriors and hating them and thinking of how I would seduce them since I was old enough to know my fate. What Maddega said of them, which was little, didn't matter. She got away. I could also. But now they had sent a woman, well, they couldn't fool me, I could learn, I could invent their pleasures as I had those of old men. To keep from remembering Maddega would be hardest, but her memory would also make it easier to get to this one – I was made in their image, after all, and I had practised.

She bargained for me with tokens for food, as is the custom, and the ceremony was silent. Maddega stood at the edge of the forest, watching. She must have escaped from the prairie to come back to the broken land, for the treaties say that what they take from us they will never send back.

'Oh, that is true enough,' Maddega said once. 'You will never return to what you are now.'

'That's too easy. Everybody gets old,' I said.

'That's a blessing,' she said. 'Having to do it the other way would be too terrible.'

So she made a shirt of soft tree leather. She said it will last half my life.

'What about the other half?' I said.

'You are responsible for that yourself,' she said, and made a pattern of flowers on the yoke. Some are dopa blossoms, and I pointed them out, laughing.

'They'll remind you of your beginnings,' she said, and twined a shape in leaves around them, a shape like a woman's centre, and said, 'That's to remind you that you were born.'

'Thanks,' I said with a sneer, but she just looked at me.

So she made me a shirt, and when at the correct time in the ceremony I had the shift removed and was washed, she came with a soft cloth to dry me, and with her rough-textured gentle hands helped me dress. The dopa distracting me, I'd been given too much for the occasion, to keep me quiet of course, and I was lost in the sensation of the shirt falling across my skin, and forgot even in her hug that I was losing her forever.

Breaking the rule of silence, she whispered into my ear, 'Goodbye for now.' For now? Am I to escape too?

'Shh,' she said. 'Go with my sisters. Sleep.'

IV

The second warrior woman met us down the path. She too rode a long, thin mount and led pack animals which had the same small feet. She took my bundles from the back of my saddle, loaded them onto a burden beast. My horse was valley-bred, with shod feet on stocky legs. She saw me looking at the feet of the other horses.

'We got these at the high pass,' she said. 'Bred for mountain crossings. They were a fine gift.' Her accent was strange; she was from the lowlands.

She turned to look fully at me, flipping long white-blonde hair back across her shoulders, and I saw with shock that her eyes were two colours, one brown, one blue. She watched me steadily, the long hands folded on the hilt of her knife which hung from her tree-leather belt, those eyes hardly blinking.

The other, the one in mail and sword belt, was older and her face was lined and wise. Even, I would say, gentle were it not that she is the warrior chief. Even with the chain mail the village elders made me put on after the ritual bath, I couldn't live like they do.

I was just the sacrificial lamb, staked outside the houses for the wolves to steal, and they stole me.

The warrior chief slipped down from her horse, and began to strip off her uniform. 'Take off that crazy armour,' she said. 'We don't like them boiled in their shells.'

I did what I was told, and stood there with the singlet dangling from my hand, Maddega's shirt caught in folds by the wind so that the sweat on my breasts and back chilled.

'Ach, leave it there,' she said. I dropped the mail shirt. 'Come along.'

There was something wrong with the distance to my beast, but I travelled it, reached for the saddle horn, reached a foot up to the stirrup, managed to get on. With the reins slack, my beast followed hers without question. Like me, a docile product of the village, walking stodgily into hell.

'It's not that bad,' said the fey-eyed one, laughing a little, and I realized I had spoken not just thought. Must not speak. Be quiet. They probably kill the noisy ones.

She laughed fully, throwing back her head. The warrior chief was further down the path, looked back.

'Alban,' said the fey one, 'this one thinks we'll eat her.'

'Why not?' said Alban, and grinned.

My mount drew up to theirs where they had stopped, and stopped also, and I fell away from the saddle, seeing the sun bright above me, then feeling it explode inside me with a jolt as my back hit the ground. The blaze above me was cut by the swing of light hair. Both of them, bending over me.

'Are you hurt?'

A fly upside down on packed earth, I could buzz but not

get up. The heads swaying in front of the sun, away. The faces in dark shadow so I could not see whose eyes were two colours. Hands testing my bones for fractures, my legs and arms for function.

'No problem,' I said dreamily, 'no problem.'

'Sal, she's stoned.'

'Can't be. It's the shock.'

'Come on, she's been riding since she was a child. Look at her pupils. That's wrong for concussion. She's doped right up.'

'Yes, of course,' I said reasonably. 'I always am.'

'Dopa, here?'

'We can get horses, they can surely get dopa through the passes.'

'We'll have to carry her. She's into the first stage. Damn it, I wish we could have talked with Maddega. This strong silent warrior crap. . .'

'Let's get going,' said the more practical one. They did not have far to carry me to their tents, which were pitched on a wide place by a stream. I knew the place, for I had played there often. We were still very close to the village.

Their voices were indistinct around me for a while, then the demons started to walk into the camp. One, one, one, one. Just a little irritating beat out of step. Coming for me to take me to the lowlands. Low lands. Away.

Blood used to buy them off, but before I could look for something sharp there were arms around me, a warmth along my back. A voice saying, sleep, little one, I'll keep the devils at bay.

V

Waking up alone in the tent. Disoriented. Everything seeming too silken. Including the warrior woman with the two-colour eyes, who sat cross-legged near the tent flap, watching me. Her hair was brushed smooth and hanging down on

either side of her thin face. She was wearing silk pants slit
on the sides so that her bony knees showed, and a silk tunic
belted with that soft leather, but she no longer had the knife.
Why is she so soft when she guards the door?

'Good, you are awake,' she said. 'Maddega is here.'

I tried to sit up, but could feel my head explode. She
picked up a cup and brought it to me. 'Here,' she said,
'drink. It'll help.'

I shook my head.

'Maddega brought it for you,' she said.

It's a trick, I thought. Shook my head again (hurt my
head). She turned her head to the door, and shouted (hurt
my ears): 'Maddega!'

'What is it, sister?' It's her voice. It's her face, poking
around the edge of the tent flap, winking at me, grinning.

'Tell your little sparrow that this isn't poison.'

Maddega laughed. Flushing, I looked away.

'Never mind,' said Maddega. 'It's a tea of dopa flowers.
It helps withdrawal. I made it for you. But you can trust
Sal, you know. When I first met her she was in worse shape
than you are. It passes. Drink it and go to sleep. You've
had an overdose again, you know.'

'I know that,' I said. 'I'm not stupid.'

'Prove it,' said Maddega, and withdrew, and I snatched
the cup and drank it.

'You must have captured her again,' I said, involuntarily.
Sal looked at me, then went out herself as I heard from
outside the tent Maddega laughing again. 'Pay attention,'
she called to me. 'You're not in the village now.' In her
voice there was a happiness – yes, happiness, what else to
call it? – which I had seldom heard, except for one day on
the alpine meadow when we went gathering herbs, and I
was almost happy myself.

The drug in a drink works fast. I cannot even finish the
memory. I sleep to the sound of Sal's voice: 'Why are they
sending us little hostile addicts now?'

VI

Maddega:

'Addicted and cruelly treated, but I have tried to take care of her since they brought her to me for training two years ago. I have tried to gentle her, but it is like handling a ferret, she'll scurry up your arm to nuzzle your neck and when you let down your guard she'll bite your breast. They surely know how to make anger in those villages. If they made progress as fast we'd have high edifices of wonder in the passes, spiderwebs of delight across the valleys. But instead they take an orphan, sterilize her, teach her to play sex games before she has her courses. Then they're delighted to keep the treaty, sending someone they know will bite. Is it their hate that shaped her? Are they what we make of them, savage counterpoint to our soft prairie ways?

'Listen to me say our, when I was born among them as she was. But I was younger, and whole and strong, and had father and mother who loved me and fed me well. What can you do with frightened ferrets raised in the wilderness, who've learned to bite when they suckle?

'Yet I've loved her, sisters, and I made sure they sent her when they might have become afraid and changed their minds. She deserves escape more than I ever did, though she wants it far less.

'I'm tired, sisters, tired here. Before long I must come home, to be renewed. I need a holiday from this despair, it's infectious and besides, insidious, if one gets used to it. I'm getting used to it.

'Spiderwebs are cruel capturing things. No, I don't wish for webs, I wish for wings to carry the young above any edifice or artifice this planet, or any other planet, can create.

'Take care of her, my dears, and safe journey.'

VII

The warrior woman stands on the hill with the west wind in her hair; she is a long way from home. She looks a strange animal in this mountain country, where the valleys are in shadow half the year. She wants the prairie wind instead of this mountain zephyr. She wants to be at home in her weathered house with this west wind blowing around the eaves. She leans her hands on the trees on either side of her and supports her weight on them, leans into the wind perilously, swings back and forth. Her hair is tangling but she doesn't notice; the wind clears her face and forces her skin to feel.

A stealthy sound behind her, a snapped twig. She turns and finds the child – she thinks 'child' though on the prairies seventeen is a time when adulthood is celebrated – closer behind her than she expects, but she does not start back.

'It's you,' she says.

'Yes,' says the girl. Her black hair is short and tumbled by the wind. She is smiling but the smile has no warmth in it. 'May I sit here with you?'

'Of course,' says Alban, then wonders if that will sound rude to the child.

'Your hair is all tangled, may I comb it?' says the girl.

'Fine,' says Alban. She likes having her hair combed, and the girl is gentle, sitting behind her and untangling the wind knots. She relaxes, leans back against the girl's knees. The girl opens her legs and hikes her backside closer, until Alban cannot imagine how she has room to comb the long hair. After a moment of feeling the girl's warmth leaned against her, it occurs to Alban – she can't imagine why it took so long to catch on – that the girl is trying to arouse her.

'I have a lover,' she says, eyes still closed. She feels the hands clench lightly around her hair, then release, then carry on.

'And I don't want another,' she continues. 'And I think it's dishonest of you to try me on, when you only want freedom.'

The hands clench again, harder, pulling her hair a little. Alban reaches back and grabs a wrist, opens her eyes and turns to face the girl.

'You can leave us any time,' she says, 'and return to the village, if you think it is such a wonderful place.'

The girl's dark face is stubbornly closed. Alban lets her anger show a little more: 'But don't try to suck me in. I'm not stupid.'

The girl is still silent in the strong grip. Alban feels hopeless. She feels that nothing she says gets through the wall. She feels the girl pull back but she will not let go, stubborn herself. 'And next time you want to comb my hair –'

'Yes, what?'

'– do it because you like me, that's all.'

She relaxes her grip and the girl twists free and runs. But she runs back to the camp.

I'm getting old, Alban thinks. *I can't get excited by children any more. They look too young. When I was seventeen, I thought I'd seen the world.*

VIII

Before I got to the camp, I stopped for breath and to wait until my face felt cool. Stupid to let the bitch get to me. Stupid to be embarrassed. But still, I did feel stupid, caught like a child at mischief. Hand slapped, taught manners, made small. How dare she preach at me? But it did hurt, like the truth always did from Maddega, though I seldom let it show. And I wouldn't let it show this time either. I was stuck with them until the flatlands, but they wouldn't see me give in.

The one with the two-colour eyes was sitting in front of the tent, laying out cards from a big deck onto the ground. She was wearing that silk tunic again, the sleeves not long enough for her long arms. Knobbly wrists, knobbly knees, wonder she didn't look blue as a bird with the autumn chill.

She has no grace, I thought, but her hands gave me the lie. She shuffled the cards, laid them again in the same pattern. When she saw me watching, she made a pass with her hand like a shaman over the deck, said, 'You will go on a long journey, into the prairie, meet a tall handsome stranger, and have many children.'

I laughed, to show I knew she mocked me. 'I won't have children.' Reluctantly, under her gaze, continued, 'That was taken out.'

'I saw the scars. Thought it was just a tubal.'

Why tell her? But I did. 'No, they took the uterus. To play a joke on the prairie warriors – and to stop me ever having anyone to care for. . . ' Shouldn't have said that, too close.

Her face darkened. She put her finger on one of the cards. 'This one.'

'What?'

'Never mind. He will have to answer for breaking the treaty. We can't ensure that the recruits come to us emotionally healthy, but at least we can legislate your physical wholeness. For your own good, though I'm sure you don't believe me.'

She put the row of four cards beside the circle, and the pattern was complete. 'What did you do?'

'Nothing, they just did it.'

'I don't mean to them, I mean for them. They must have had a reason.'

'I was a whore.' I used the low dialect word defiantly, purposely, but when her face got even angrier it seemed it was not at my semantics.

'They still train children for that?'

'I'm no child, I'm seventeen.'

'And have done the job for how long?'

'Five years, on and off.'

'So you began at twelve.'

'Almost thirteen,' I said. She laid the rest of the cards deliberately on the ground, rose in a single motion without using her hands. She is taller than I am, though I was the tallest in the village. They are both taller than I am.

'On the prairies a child gets ready for her coming-of-age at seventeen. If she plays at sex before then, it is with her peers; after then it is with whomever she chooses. Adults who take a child against her will, by force or manipulation, are ostracised and she is cherished until she can put it behind her. She has not been cut apart already for years, made a convenience for the use of a village and fed dopa to keep her pliable.'

'And who services the hungry people?'

'Other adults, by choice. Lovers. Friends.'

'And does this work? I suppose you have no rape, no fetishists, no weird preferences there on the perfect prairie?'

Her hands were on my shoulders. 'Sometimes we have anger. But we do not make our children into mules with twisted souls. You think we come for children because we need an army on the prairie? We have had no war, no "soldiers", for a hundred years. We take you to get you out of there, and to send you back with hearts. You think Maddega, who went back two years ago, is old? Or that she's finished her life's work? It has just started. No more children will be neutered in your village, if she has to get rid of that twisted old head councillor herself.' She was shaking me.

'Ah, you kill, you holy lowlanders?' I asked her through gritted teeth.

'I didn't. . . Yes. Yes, we kill. With kindness.' She let me go and bent to pick up her cards. 'I have taken away your dopa and burned it,' she added. 'We have no dopa on the prairie. This is the world. Learn to like it.'

She walked away from me through the autumn grass, swaying like a reed herself. Near the trees the other one stood. She went to her, they talked, looking back at me, then they put each an arm around the other and walked into the trees, the taller one bending her head under branches.

IX

They send us little sparrows with their wings clipped. How do they think they will fly? They send us little birds with banded legs. The history of her life is tattooed on her hip, I have discovered, to be read when she is used, like a gypsy burden beast. Worse, for the burden beasts otherwise have a soft kind of life.

Alban is angry but she says little, so as not to bruise my feelings. She has seen this before, but last time the drug was taken in a different way, and it was in a country far to the west, and there was no treaty, and she and I stole away in the night with true daring, none of this sham to play the game of a fifty-year-old phony diplomacy.

X

Going to sleep that night was only difficult because of what I feared waking up might be. The two women fed me, and I ate, though I loathed their kindness, knew it for false. Then I lay down in the tent, refusing to speak, and pulled the furry blanket over me. I tried to keep myself awake, tried to think of where I might get more dopa, could not think of any answer that didn't mean going back to the village. And that I swore I would never do, whatever they did to me.

Gradually I slept, drifted away, down the long dark river that flowed through the camp, down to a cool white sea. At the edge of sleep I heard them talking outside the tent, and had a momentary clear thought before the whiteness swallowed me. I thought: *These women act as they choose. I have nothing to give them but a face damped down by the dopa. No wonder Alban won't have me and Sal will not smile, though I planned for them to find me attractive.*

XI

When I started to wake there was no one there, then I felt a body. *She is the one who keeps the drug from me. I think I know how to kill her.* I turned as if for sex, but I reached for the neck instead of the groin. Her soft hands were iron against my wrists, holding my arms to the ground, her body clad in silk on top of my naked body, her legs pinning mine down. *Maybe I can get her off. Arc and struggle. Arch and writhe away.* She was taller, had the advantage, held me. She swore, soft voice, must have been the one with two-colour eyes. Sal. But she felt as kind as the other. Both of them are softer than I am. Which was it? Everything was soft but she wouldn't let me get away. Her face came down; she held my head still by pressing her cheek against mine, pinning me so that I couldn't keep up the rhythmic pounding of my head backwards against the ground. Everything soft, her hair against my eyes.

She said, 'I won't let you hurt. Try me all you want.'

'You must like this. Like pressing all over me.'

'Don't make me laugh,' she said. 'Touching bodies isn't all sex.'

I pushed against her, gasping now for breath. 'Fucking is like this.'

'No. Controlled . . . violence . . . to make someone leave you alone in the end?'

'Except . . . ' I said, discovering that if I twisted my arm I could reach her with an elbow, try to gouge myself free.

'Except what?' She pinned my elbow with hers.

' . . . with Maddega.'

'Bet she asked first.'

'Yes.' I got a knee free, angled it to her groin. She pushed her body down, between my knees, so I couldn't hurt her. I had a free leg to flail across her back, but there was only her soft ass to kick. 'Damn you! Too soft.'

She laughed unexpectedly. 'Not time yet when I'd let you kick me for pleasure.' She held both my hands with one of hers, with the other captured the leg, pushed it down and tucked her own across to hold it.

'Leave me alone.'

'No, baby, I can't.'

'Not a baby.'

'I know. Never mind. This part only lasts a few . . . a little while. Need to eat? Crap?'

'No. Need to . . .'

'What?'

'Fight.' But under her restraint I could relax until there was relative peace. I was safe in my anger; this was a kind prison. I drifted away.

In the night, the true night, I felt her move off me, away from me. My freed body reached for the sky, the tent wall, her, and I fell into sleep again, a real sleep, the kind with dreams. I dreamt about having a lover, with eyes of two colours, who takes me into the hills, and I lie down with him on mountain ledges, make love, fall, fall, fall.

XII

If I didn't know how much anger was condensed into that small frame I'd pity her, looking crumpled and sweating there, asleep for the moment, a lull in the storm.

There's a wind comes across the mountains to the prairie in winter. By the time it reaches the spaceport it is dry, and it sucks the prairie dry; suddenly snow is gone and temperatures rise. But so do tempers, and people suffer depressions, and there are even, sometimes, suicides among the young. When you have no experience, it seems so hopeless to be sucked so dry so quickly, as if the water cycle will never turn again. The warm winter sunshine then speaks of death as well as life. I think of the warm wind as I watch her sleep. Uneasy tossing. Any moment she could wake violent or passive or screaming in pain. Or self destructive,

I suppose, looking at those arms, but I have no experience with that.

And she is awake, watching me ferally. No other move.

'You're awake again,' I say. 'I hope the dreams were not too bad. They are only dreams.'

Her words are slurred. 'You . . . your eyes . . . different colours? Why?'

'Don't know. But the doctors say I'm lucky not to be deaf. It goes together, in kittens.'

'Very strange. Very . . . strange. What does it mean?'

'Nothing. It's just my eyes.'

'In my dream. Eyes.'

'My eyes were in your dream? Was it good dreaming?'

She begins to experiment like a child. Head rolling back and forth. Raises a hand and watches her fingers spread and turn. 'Why does it still work?'

'What?'

'The world. Should stop. Why not?'

She looks at her scarred arm. 'I tried to stop it. Won't let me. Why not let me? Why not let me? Let me go.' And by the end is yelling again, and leaps up, leaps for the spoon in the stew bowl still here from my lunch.

There would be certain irony, I recognize as I hold the point of the spoon away from her arm, in telling her at this point that she is free, if she could only see it. So I merely hold her so she can't hurt herself, then so she can't hurt me as she fights back, then herself again as she throws herself down and backwards and tries to bash her head on the tent poles. Luckily her motion is not as compulsive as that first terrible pounding of her head against the ground, which jarred me to the base of my spirit.

Finally I have her pinned on the bedroll again, and she fights each time my resistance is relaxed past a certain point, fights to make sure I hold her down. I remember this state too well, and I hold her wrists tightly, her arms crossed in front of her body; I'm sitting on her thighs so she can't keep kicking at me.

'Damn,' she says, 'you soft people are so hard to fight.'

Can't help laughing, and she says, 'You always laugh at me.'

'You don't know, little bird. What a turnaround. Me here with you like this.'

'Maddega said . . . you were worse?'

'Distilled dopa, by vein all the time. Not just eating it like you. Seven years for the cells to replace and the body to go clean.'

'So you know.'

'Seven years of demons. I know.'

'Still, no guarantee. Why trust you? Even your eyes go two ways.'

'Can't help that. Born that way. You're a brown girl. So?' All this while exerting pressure against each other. Isometric exercise.

'I suppose. But.'

And quiet. Slowly, as she relaxes, I relax also. My hands cramp as soon as I do and I wait without moving until the muscles relax. It's rather calm, for the moment. Time for the next step.

'Look, I'm hungry,' I say. 'Ten minutes break. Can you handle it alone that long, no cuts, no bites, no pounding and kicking?'

She thinks. 'Maybe.'

'How can I know with "maybe"?'

'Five minutes?'

In answer I call, 'Alban!' Alban at the tent flap. 'I need food ready so I can take a break. Fine?'

'Fine.' I hear her at the fire, hear the clink of bowl and spoon. When she brings the bowl in I start to let go.

'Not her! Not her!' says the girl, and Alban nods, sets down the bowl of stew, and goes out. I get up, massaging fingers and stretching shoulders. Pick up the bowl and eat, glancing at her seldom but aware every moment.

'Are you hungry yet?'

Shakes her head too hard. I can see her stop herself.

Hands carefully clasped in her lap. Legs crossed. Soon she is holding her feet in clenched fingers. Holding onto what she has promised. I take the disputed spoon, last meal's bowl and this one's, and put them outside. Alban reaches out from her seat by the fireside to touch my face.

It's night and the world has shrunk to a fire, a badly-lit tent, a blonde woman outside, a dark child inside. I am half of each, a blue eye for Alban, a brown eye for the little sparrow, I am divided into dark and light down a fine line, and I go back into the tent.

She is holding her wrists each with the other clamping hand as if restraining herself. Every muscle tense.

'Tomorrow you'll be hungry,' I say, as she exchanges her own control for mine.

'Promise?'

'Yes. Try to sleep for a while.'

A long time after she tucks herself against me, I feel the wrap of tension slide from her small body. Not so small, just smaller than me. Alban in the night puts a cover over us and moves the lantern so I wake to a comforting warm brownness for a while, adjust the covers around the still sleeping child, and again sleep myself.

XIII

Blood already dripping from her arm. She cut into the fleshy part, for scars not suicide. Where did she get the blade? Where did she get the dopa? Blood.

Alban has left it to me, after one look at us went away and started cleaning up the chaos the sparrow had made of the camp. Should I thank her? Blood. And up to me.

A strip from my tunic. Silk won't tear. Luckily I caught my sleeve on a branch earlier; I rip from that spot across. Something clean to bind beneath it, the cloth I had readied for my courses. Go toward her.

She's bleeding on my blankets. Why retreat to my bed?

'You're bleeding,' I say. 'Let me tie this on it.'

'It needs to be stitched,' she says.

'Now? Who can do it?'

'Maddega used to do it.'

'I've no kit.'

'Use Alban's.'

She is looking at me from narrowed calculating eyes. I know why Maddega's ferret description. The hostility stops me. I almost rise to it but good sense intervenes and I lower my tense shoulders. Breathe. Say:

'I don't know how.'

'I can do it.' She is still testing me. I rummage for Alban's first aid kit (interesting that she knew it was there), pull out sticky bandages. 'Here. These work too.' Butterfly-shaped tape.

'Has to be cleaned.' But I see she is no longer holding her arms out in that awkward challenging way. She has pulled them in toward her belly. Bleeds on her own clothes now. Small comfort.

'Hurry,' she says, 'it's starting to wear off.'

Alban says I look coldest when I'm terrified. If so, ice is good for bleeding wounds. I never cut or burned myself as she has done. My own arms ache.

'Where did you get it?'

'The dopa tea Maddega gave you.'

'I thought you had finally agreed to stop.'

'It's my business.'

I have wet the cloths with water from the basin, into which I've poured disinfectant from the bottle in Alban's kit. Sparrow huddles even further back against the tent wall. I have to take the basin to her. The water careens off the sides of the basin. As I put it down a wave slops out onto the blankets.

'Damn.'

I reach for her wrist, straighten her arm. She flinches. 'It hurts.' She sounds surprised.

'Of course, silly sparrow. It's deep.'

'It doesn't usually hurt yet.'

'Yes, well, when?'

'Later. And only aches.'

'You were almost withdrawn. Weeks without it. No level in your system. One dose won't do the trick.'

She closes her eyes. Her face is pale now, she is beginning to shiver. I have finished cleaning the blood but as she shivers my fingers, holding the wound, keep slipping.

'Hold still,' I say, and she manages to still herself long enough for me to put on the butterfly tapes. They hold the wound shut, thank goodness, so I will not have to do my first sewing in human flesh. After a moment she opens her eyes.

'I've never seen those,' she whispers.

'Technology has its benefits,' I say.

'I'm sorry,' she says, and begins to cry.

'Do you have any idea what you want?' I say. I daub a clean bandage with salve and wrap her forearm. Another strip makes an adequate sling.

'No,' she says.

'And will dopa bring it?'

'I'd have to go . . . back to the mountains. You said . . . you have no dopa on the plains.' She is shivering and holding herself curled and tight, but I swear she's trying to grin.

'You bloody fool,' I say, 'look at my quilts.' As I pull the wet and stained top quilt away, wrap all the rest around her, push her down until she lies curled on her side. I put the basin down on the ground, gather the kit together, move to get up. She reaches out with her other arm, grasps my wrist.

'Don't go,' she says. 'Sorry, don't.'

'I'll be back in a minute,' I say, 'You can last.' Her grip desperate. 'I won't be out of sight, I promise.' She lets go. I return the kit to Alban's bag, hook the wet quilt across two tent poles so it can dry. Pull one of Alban's blankets onto my bed, pull off my pants and socks and get into bed beside her. Tuck the blankets around us both. She's tense.

'You'll be fine,' I say, 'don't worry.'

'Can't,' she says. 'Too cold.'

'I told you. . . '

'Can't worry. Thanks. Sorry. Sorry.'

'Shut up. You can apologize later. Better still, you can get the blood out of my quilt tomorrow. Right?'

'Deal.'

'Sleep,' I say. Hold her shivering close. She is a long time warming. She's in shock. Finally her breathing deepens and widens to encompass sleep. When I find time to sleep myself, I dream of strange accidents and omens, the kinds of dreams I'd be glad not to remember.

'Wrong,' she says sharply in the middle of the night.

'What?' I'm disoriented, awakening from a dream of difficulty.

'If it doesn't take the pain away, why use it? If it hurts anyway?' She seems asleep, says no more, and I sleep again, thinking before I do, I wish I were holding Alban. Or Alban were holding me. I am tired from sparrow battles, could use some comforting myself.

In the night Alban tends the fire, and we are all warm by morning.

XIV

'It's time to ride on,' said Alban, and Sal nodded.

'We're seven weeks late already,' she said. 'Transport won't have waited, but we can go with the gypsies.'

'We'll pass the towns after the roads close for winter.'

'They'll let us by, coming this way. Down, not up.'

I had no idea what this was about, except that it meant I would be able to move my restless body. The bandage itched and I picked at the edge.

'Leave that alone,' said Sal sharply, and went out of the tent. Alban looked at me and smiled. I followed Sal.

She was packing bundles, getting them ready for the pack

animal. I watched her lanky economy of motion. So different from Maddega's plump bustling or Alban's sparse grace.

How does anyone accept what they can't have? Can't get? Not easy. First I couldn't get a good life, but dopa helped with that. Now I couldn't get dopa, but I decided that was just my body, I didn't want the drug after all, learned to swim up from that constant haze – and only found more frustration. Found nerve endings I never knew – and never knew would vibrate and clamour so much for a return touch. Sal was as impersonal as Maddega when she'd tend my scars after a beating. I wanted to hold her forever. When she turned to the fire, I put myself in her way.

She took my arms from around her neck. 'Stand on your own,' she said. 'Am I your crutch?' That was no answer.

'I'm good at it. I know how.'

'I know you've started feeling. Start thinking too. Otherwise it washes you away.'

'How would you know?'

'Arrogant little sparrow. You think you can tell me anything new about my old enemy? I told you it took me seven years. Maybe it will be the same for you, even though you only ate it. Seven years to get in balance, and even then you live your life with all the same brain cells.'

'But I want –'

'Seven years to freedom,' she said relentlessly, 'and the way to go isn't to get addicted to me instead, even if I wanted you hanging on me day and night.'

'Don't you –?'

'If I wanted a pet,' she said, 'I'd get a cat, not train a child to the leash. You're too used to licking wrists when you aren't biting them.' And she walked back into the tent.

Folds of silk fell across behind her. Bitch. Every time I tried to do what they told me to do, they turned me down. Or around. But the disgust was not just at her. Me. She was right. Trading one master for another was not the way. And it didn't help me to know it, just made me horribly aware of a long hard future.

The other one played good to Sal's bad. 'You all right?'

'Shut up,' I said, and went off to split the next morning's wood. When I came back they were in bed, and I stood outside the tent for a moment, listening to them murmur and giggle. I did not think I could sleep next to that. But I was very tired.

The next day as we rode I realized that I had lost more to the drug than my detachment. My muscles were weak. They put me on a tall pony and used my small horse for packs. Riding eventually became a torment. But I am a mountain rider, and instead of admitting my stiffness I turned surly. They were not so wonderful that they resisted teasing me. We rode through towns I would have otherwise wanted to see in a thick mist that was partly in the world, partly in my angry mind. When the pack horse threw a shoe and they began to worry about finding a smithy, then I could smile. But it seemed cold comfort that now all of us were miserable.

XV

Halfway down the escarpment that separates the inland counties from the prairie, Alban realizes that Sparrow is worried. She rides without her habitual scowl, but instead with an ear turned to their back trail.

Finally she says, 'I think there's someone following us.' After she says it, Alban realizes that it has been a struggle for her to speak, but that fear finally overcame pride.

'Yes,' Alban says, 'since about midday.'

'You knew?' A mixture of irritation and relief made the young one's voice a study.

'Yes, I have been hearing the hoof-beats for a while.'

'Shouldn't we be wary?'

'In the inland counties, it's likely to be a friend.' Then she sees Sparrow's face looking naked and ready to cry. 'Child, what is it?'

'I thought it was from the drug. Like the demons that used to walk.' And she does cry, slightly and perhaps unconsciously.

Alban reins her horse back so she rides beside the child's mount, leans over and touches her shoulder. 'No,' she says, 'You were right. You heard it. Eventually you will learn that you can trust yourself now.'

A few minutes later the sounds resolve into a small man on a small horse emerging from the dapple of sun through leaves. 'You are very late,' he calls.

'You are hasty,' calls Sal familiarly, and all but Sparrow laugh. The prairie women know him well.

'We'll make camp,' says Alban. 'This is our friend.' Hearing each other described so economically, both Sparrow and the man smile.

XVI

The small dark man moves around the fire. He has small, neat hands compared with the long knotty fingers of the fey-eyed woman. He is preparing dinner, she is putting up tents. Every now and then she touches those long fingers to the back of his hand, his back, his waist as they move around the campsite.

His hands are busy among the knives, pots and dishes. She has plenty to do far from the campfire. Yet they move past each other often, they touch often. Watching them, Sparrow thinks they are foolish, so different in size and shape. How could a man so small want a woman like her? Yet when supper is ready and Alban has taken plates for herself and the girl, he serves two plates and takes one to Sal, who thanks him with a dazzling smile. Sparrow has never seen such a smile from Sal, she is moved despite herself to watch them without prejudice. They even share their food. In Sparrow's village this is taboo but she has seen Alban and Sal do it unthinkingly. This sharing of food between Sal and the small man, however, is not humdrum; they are making love with each gift.

Finally they put the plates aside and he touches her face so softly that Sparrow is frightened, he seems dangerous. Sal only bends her head into his touch and turns her mouth into his palm. She takes his hand and they get up and go into one of the tents, which Sparrow now sees has been set up just outside the circle of firelight.

She feels as if she has been watching through a window, something very private taking place. Only then she thinks of Alban and turns to her.

'Makes you hungry, doesn't it, little one,' says Alban idly. She's peeling an apple carefully.

'What about you?' blurts Sparrow. 'She's yours.'

'Not mine. Just with me. She makes love with him across the foot of my bed.'

'What do you mean?'

'It's what we say on the prairies when we don't mind. It's good to watch, isn't it? Feels good.'

'Good? Aren't you angry?'

'That village is a wicked place,' says Alban, and throws down the peel of her apple. It lands in a long double curl. 'My love is an S,' she says, grinning. 'Sal?'

'Sparrow?'

Alban looks at her, the grin fades. Hands on Sparrow's shoulders. 'You want what they have tonight,' she says, 'not what I have. I want it too, but not from you. Thanks anyway, but go to sleep, little one.'

Sparrow makes to pull away in anger but Alban holds on, turns her again to face her. 'I said thanks,' she says, 'I meant it. I am flattered, but it's not the night. It's not right to mistake one kind of longing for another.'

'But how to get comfort?' Sparrow cries out in desperation. Alban looks at her more gently still.

'I will hold you if you want comfort, but that's not what making love is for. Come here,' she says, and takes the small body close to her. Sparrow's arms hold her reluctantly.

Alban laughs gently. 'Relax,' she says, and chuckles. Sparrow hugs her more tightly, pulls back and means to kiss her. With one hand Alban holds the girl's head against her shoulder. 'Shhh,' she says, 'shhh. You'll grow into it, it's all right.'

After Alban tucks Sparrow into bed she sits beside her, calming her by stroking her hair. Finally, just as the little one is approaching sleep, a tear rolls from the corner of each closed eye. Alban leaves one hand on the dark hair until she's certain the young one sleeps, then goes to her own bed to sleep curled around her fist which she has pressed against her groin. She wakes once in the night to find she has opened up in sleep; she is sprawled on her back with the cover half off and her hand outflung and opened to the cool air.

When she wakes again, it is the cool grey light of predawn and Sal is standing above her, the silk garments whispering as she draws them off. Alban opens the bed to her and Sal slides in, her body cool where it meets Alban's warmth.

'Fine?' says Alban sleepily.

'Mmm-hmm,' says Sal. 'He's heading back home. Has to be at some kind of meeting.'

'Mmm,' says Alban, and pulls Sal against her and into sleep.

XVII

The next day I was so irritable that even I knew it had to be something more. These women were getting to me. Even if I didn't want to trust them, I was starting to believe what they did. Maybe even what they said. I wanted someone to put a warm hand against my face, love me like that, so gently. The night before, as Alban stroked my hair, I tried to keep hating her, for what she was and for making my wanting seem foolish. But she had been so kind, and she was right, I didn't want her, really. And her hand was so gentle, comforting me. I wanted, and how I wanted, simple comfort and love. Why had I been put in that village with the pain and the drug and the work I hated so much, making all those old men happy? While Alban could be the chief of the warriors, and Sal had two lovers who even seemed like friends.

Friend. What a rusty word that was on my tongue. Thinking of it the night before, tears I usually could conquer had won their way into the night. I felt them roll down my temples, but not reach my hair; out of such a tiredness that I hardly could bear it, I fell asleep.

So I was irritable. Everything was wrong. I didn't want to snarl at Alban but I had lost something the night before and she had seen it go. It took a while for that to occur to me. When it did I was angrier than ever, not knowing whether to be ashamed of myself or hate even more the life I had left which had made me what I am.

Finally I couldn't bear it. Sal was not gloating, but her face looked so peaceful, even more than usual. Alban and she touched and smiled and seemed happier together also. Everything I had learned was wrong, and I would always be alone. I put down the bundle I was packing and ran out of the camp. I heard them looking for me, but I hid and hoped they could not find me. And hoped they would look harder, and find me. Or someone would find me.

It wasn't my fault, I thought, and cried and cried, curled under a thicket of bushes where I stayed until I felt a spider crawling on my leg, and opened my eyes to find it in front of my face, about to move from my knee to my nose. I could not control the cry of revulsion, the sudden leaping away I made.

And that is how Sal found me, still crying, brushing the leaves and fallen bark off my clothes, terrified that more spiders crawled there, half-blind with a fear that even in extremity I knew was stupid.

She put her arms around me. I began to scream.

'Shh, shh,' she said. 'You're safe now.' And she put her hands on my head, quieting me.

'I don't believe you,' I said. 'I don't believe you.'

'It doesn't matter,' she said. 'You will learn.'

The next day we came to the bottom of the escarpment and rode out of the forests onto a wide flat freedom that they said was the prairie. We camped there a while, and I began to get used to the wind, the sky and the space. Then the creaking bright wagons of the gypsies came and took us to the spaceport.

War and Rumours of War

I

The women rode through at dusk on their small-footed mountain horses. From the door of his workshop he watched them pass, three strangers in the caps and cloaks of the prairies, but only two were prairie folk. He knew that because only two had long hair, caught into plaits at the back of the neck. They were both blonde, but the third was dark-skinned and small in the manner of the mountain folk, and her hair was short under her cap, and her expression was a scowl.

The three horses being ridden placed their feet with precision, but he noticed that the pack horse was limping.

He watched them until they vanished into the mist, listened until the jingling of their harnesses faded into the general noises of the Market below. Just at that edge of audibility, he fancied, he heard one speak and the others laugh richly in reply.

Wake up, there's work to do, he thought, shook himself,

and went back to his workbench. Today he was making a delicate forgery, copying a silver buckle set with carnelian, the badge of authority of a semi-royal house in a neighbouring county. The job should pay well.

As he worked he thought of the women, of why the prairie people went into the highlands in the summer. The dark one must be their new sister. Didn't look too happy to be chosen.

But prairie warriors so late in the year? It was already mist season, and the short snowfalls of early autumn had clogged the grasses more than once, though none of the snow had yet survived the midday sun. But in all his years in this inland city, he had never seen the warriors pass this late. He began to consider what would delay a small group of warriors for a few weeks between the mountain passes and the base of the hills.

He was just then carving the coat of arms of a semi-royal house onto a cabochon of carnelian, and he reflected that the warriors' path must have lain not far from the home estates of that very house. He wondered if they had been delayed there. Perhaps to await a message, and carry it on to allies on the prairies. That would not be unusual. But what news had to be waited for?

Only birth, or death, or war. In a sudden surge of revelation his hand almost slipped. He had seen the reason clearly, and, incredibly, his part in it. So this forgery was to be that important, was it? And Tholian had only offered him a pittance for it. He must raise the price.

He stretched and shook himself again, took up a gentle brush and swept the face of the carving clean. When his lover came looking for him an hour later, to go gambling with him in the Market, the jeweller was singing rather exuberantly, albeit with small consideration of tune.

'How is the work today?' said the intimate friend.

'My dear,' said the jeweller, 'if I am right, the work is very, very lucrative. Come, I must stop by Straight Street on the way to the game. I have a little business there, and you will be my safeguard. If I don't come out in twenty minutes, call for reinforcements and come looking for me.'

II

The being called Tholian was a human, but somehow so cool and distant from all that is human, from emotions and passions and the concerns of everyday life, that business partners would have been glad to know they had met an alien, so as not to have to admit even the slightest kinship with him. He looked coldly at the jeweller. Had the miserable man been taking lessons in deportment? He seemed to have grown.

'What exactly is it that you want? You have been full of innuendo and ellipsis since you barged in here, but you've said nothing I understand.'

'Surely what I am doing is worth more than the paltry offer you made, especially considering just how important it is that I do my work well. You know no one else in this county could pull it off. I know what is at stake here.'

'Oh, you do?' Meaning to be mocking, but realizing at the moment of utterance that it could sound as much like an admittance of ignorance as one of knowledge. Neither of which Tholian had.

'I think you should settle a larger sum on me. I want to be reasonable, since I'll no doubt be working for you in future if your plan goes well, so let's say – five thousand instead of five hundred?'

'Five thousand! Who do you think I represent that would have such a sum to spend on this kind of work?'

'Ah, but that's just the thing, isn't it? That's just the question.'

'Wait,' said Tholian, and walked across to the desk near the window, sat overlooking the Market.

If this small-time forger knew something, the Market must be crawling with rumours. What did they know that had not come first to the ears of Tholian, who usually had access to the best information at all levels? It might be worth some money to find out.

'Fine,' said Tholian without stirring. 'Five thousand is reasonable. But that includes information. Keep your ears open in the next few days. When you bring the finished work, bring some news too. If it's worthwhile I'll pay. If not, three thousand for the piece alone.'

'Four.'

'Three and a half.'

'Done. And an advance, for expenses?'

Tholian laughed (and a rather chilling production that was) and produced a gold ingot. 'Five hundred in advance.' And as the jeweller reached for it, an icy hand drew it back for a moment. 'Don't spend it all in the game tonight. And remember, I may depend on your work, but you depend on my good will, for your work to continue, for your pleasures with that sweet young thing who waits outside to continue, for your very life to continue. Don't wrong me, or you'll feel it.'

'Right-oh,' said the jeweller, who had heard that and similar warnings before.

Out on the street again, talking to the 'sweet young thing', he said, 'Cor, doesn't Tholian think we're all wise to that crap? As if we'd do business and not know the risks. There's no honour among thieves any more.'

'Was there ever?' said his friend, and they went on toward the Market, the jeweller anticipating a fine night of gambling with five hundred in gold to waste. In the window above them, Tholian sat staring at the skyline, thinking of strategies.

III

'I'm not in the mood for tricks,' Tholian shouted. 'Don't you think I know what the news is in the Market and in every inn on the outskirts? Do you think you can treat me like a child at suck?'

'Oh, calm down,' said the woman in black. 'I'm not some little underworld thug you can intimidate. I'm probably the only living person who remembers when you actually were a babe at suck, and I'm no more frightened of you now than I was then.'

'And with the obligatory putting-me-in-my-place out of the way, could you now tell me, please, just what is going on?'

'As far as I know, just what I told you. Robbery and mayhem on a very small scale. That's why such a small budget was allocated. Which, by the way, dear sib, you have exceeded considerably.'

Tholian was icy again. 'When every serf in the Marketplace is whispering about insurrection in neighbouring states, and every cretin I buy for bed has nothing to say at climax but that there will be war, what am I to do but pay to find out more? Especially when it all seems to revolve around that little piece of jewellery you have there, and the purpose for which it could be used if in fact the Regent is mad or dead.'

'Come now, if that were the case, do you think I wouldn't know?'

'You might be overestimating yourself, dear sister.'

'Hmph. Let me authorize your budget overrun, and then I'll see what I can find out. There might be money to be made from all this.'

'Precisely my thought,' said Tholian, thinking instead her robe was a most unbecoming shade. 'Have you ever thought of red, sister?'

'Red?'

'For a robe.'

She turned back to look at her younger sibling. 'Tholian, mother always said you were the oddest of her children. Are you sure we share the same father?'

And with this old joke the two parted company, returning to their own nests of intrigue.

IV

The semi-royal Regent of a semi-royal house sat in the high tower room looking out across the home estate. But not thinking of the view, though it was a spectacular one, from a five-storey height in a land where even a two-storey structure was somewhat unusual. Instead, the Regent was thinking about the news brought by the messenger who sat gasping for breath on the footstool by the semi-royal chair.

Tarot cards lay on the table, their configuration forgotten in the shock of this new knowledge. 'Tell me again,' said the Regent.

'It was noised about in the Market of an inland city with which we have trade – I'm sure you know of what place I speak – that three prairie warriors passed through covertly under cover of the mists, one with a wounded horse. It became known that they were on a secret mission for someone in this house, which kept them beyond the normal time for prairie travellers on their summer quests. A minor jeweller who has a sideline in forgery was found beaten in the Market and during his delirium he revealed he had made a replica of the semi-royal seal for a certain Tholian, a cold fish in the information business. Tholian has a sister who works for the Establishment, deputy to a major power figure. Her agents have been active in all the Markets of the inland counties. Meanwhile, the prairie women stopped at a smithy which is known to be a cover for agents of certain parties hostile to your Regency. Since then, more than one agent has heard the rumour that you, esteemed Regent, are either locked within your tower mad as a sandstorm, or dead before your Regency comes to term. This is the news from the north-west.'

'And what became of these prairie people?'

'They must have gone along their way. There are no more details in the message.'

'Damned nonsense, all of it. Why, here I am hale and healthy as the day I became Regent! Next year, when the kids come of age, and take over, I'll retire and gladly, but until then, I won't have this nonsense perpetuated. Go back and tell your people to start spreading the truth around for a change, instead of gathering lies. And tell that damned smith to cut it out. Just because he can't stand the idea that his brother could be Regent and he couldn't. Tell him if he doesn't leave me alone I'll start telling the world some secrets of his. He isn't the only one who can play politics. Tell him that. Then come back and report to me again.'

'Right away? But there is much to be done, esteemed Regent!'

The prospect of climbing all those stairs again no doubt fuels this loyal servant's reluctance, thought the Regent. 'Oh, very well. Report next week. But let's get busy on this before the rumours are too widespread to stop.'

'Yes, gracious one.'

The messenger departed, to toil back down the stairs to the main castle. The Regent tapped idly on a jewelled cuff and considered strategies, then stood and strode, brocade robes swirling, into the alcove where his carrier birds cooed in their cages. Capturing one was easy after years of practice, but as usual the Regent had forgotten to write the message first, and while doing so, only with some struggle prevented the bird from escaping prematurely. Finally one voluminous brocade sleeve became a temporary cage while the message was completed and the parchment folded. Then he inserted the message into a sheath on the rumpled bird's leg.

The Regent stood semi-regally in the window embrasure, and reaching up launched the bird on its flight. Its white form soon vanished into the clouds.

'It will be done,' the Regent murmured, nodding in satisfaction, turned again to the table, and redealt the game of solitaire the messenger had interrupted.

V

Maddega, prairie-educated wise woman of the mountains, was sitting in front of her modest hut looking down on the mountain village when the dove alighted on her shoulder. She detached the message and let the bird fly up into the spreading tree above the hut. She read the Regent's brief message, noticing the characteristically untidy calligraphy.

'No!' she said to herself, but in a tone of amusement rather than alarm, and laughed aloud. Then she went to her own desk, and on the back of the Regent's note wrote a few words. Calling down the bird again, she inserted the note into the holder.

A few words to the well-trained avian messenger sent it fleeting back into the sky. Maddega chuckled with glee as she saw it take its course not toward the semi-royal house from whence it came, but toward the lowlands.

The message should be appreciated on the prairie, she thought, and this idea kept her smiling all day.

VI

By the time the first staying snow of winter had fallen, the jeweller had stopped hoping for business from the war. If it was to come, it would come next year, when the semi-royal children (twins, he thought, but couldn't truly remember) came of age. He refused to believe the counter-rumours that said the semi-royal teenagers had wonderful dispositions and were inseparable, refusing to reign at all if they couldn't share everything.

When the twins began to bicker, as he was sure they would, there would be fireworks in the inland counties, and the fallout would be in clandestine work for him, both as an agent of Tholian's information web and as a forger of documents. His most popular forgeries in the last war he'd attended (which had been, of course, on another continent) had been discharge certificates – he had even awarded one citation for valour, and that had kept him in beer and bread all of one summer.

If he thought at all of the prairie women, it was only in bed with his lover, when they speculated ribaldly about what the prairie warriors (of both sexes) did in bed. Neither the jeweller nor his companion were in any position to know the truth, and knew it, and enjoyed the conversation a great deal as a result.

VII

Meanwhile, a caravan of three riders halted at the foot of the hills to make camp and wait for the gypsy wagons. The three women chatted together as they built a fire and prepared the meal.

'You're looking a little more limber, Sparrow,' said the fey-eyed one slyly.

'You two are never going to let me forget it, are you.'

'Forget that rare event, sore muscles from riding, on a mountain rider? Of course not!' said the other prairie woman, her lined face crinkling as she smiled. 'Besides, you were being a pain in the ass as well as having them.'

'After seven weeks of dopa withdrawal you would be too,' retorted Sparrow. 'And the pack horse losing a shoe didn't help. Having to stop at that smithy that day when I didn't want anyone to see me –'

'That smith was a strange fellow,' the older woman said reflectively, 'with all that snide gossip about his brother who was supposed to be the Regent of somewhere. I wonder why. . . ' She was interrupted by a flurry of white wings.

'Look!' cried Sparrow. 'One of Maddega's birds!' The white dove alit on her upraised hand. 'There's something in the message tube.'

Sparrow unfolded the parchment and with increasing puzzlement read the scrawled message aloud. ' "Send me the names of the three women who are causing these rumours about me. I want them stopped." '

'Untidy grammar,' commented the fey-eyed woman; 'does the sender want the women or the rumours stopped? Who wrote it? Is it in Maddega's hand?'

'No –' Sparrow turned the message over '– but this is. She's using recycled parchment again.'

The message on the other side, in Maddega's neat writing, said, 'Bring me some honey when you come next year.'

The older woman nodded and laughed. 'Just like Maddega to send a bird this far with a shopping list!' And the others laughed too, for they all knew Maddega well, and loved her better.

With that, the scrap of parchment went into the fire, the released bird flew back into the dusk, and a traveller riding by on the nearby road heard the sound of women laughing and smiled himself, thinking of the merriment he would soon share at his own hearth.

And so the story ends as it began, with the laughter of three women overheard at nightfall. It may be that some day the inland counties will shatter their hundred-years' reputation for peace, but it was not done that autumn.

Black Dog

'I like a view but I like to sit with my back to it.'

Gertrude Stein

I

Drawn to the last indistinct cravings of day like a beast to the light. What you can expect from sunset: sadness (nostalgia), flame, death of the sun, birth of night.

Night, the tranquil time of blessedness, time when the hard blue bowl is lifted, beneath which by day we labour and scurry and complain of details. Night. Freedom. Infinity. Peace.

All this a way to introduce my favourite darkness. I have learned that savagery is the province of day; daylight a cocoon from which by dark I burst, wings unfurling into the cool moonlight, silver and silk. Night is the gossamer time of reflection; night is the freedom to fly unchecked. Spread your wings, sister/brother, come speak the once-heard language of aspiration with me, search for stars and soaring flights of life.

Out on the darkling plain I stand where the smooth silver expanse of the snowy field begins. No one larger than the black dog has been there this winter; the dog capers dark across the blankness like a cut-out into a deeper night.

If I am ready to live alone now, I am not ready for complete solitude. Up there in the stars I read the history of my far-flung travelling friends; they are so far away, and the dog and I stand on this snow-field, freed, watching their gleaming traces in the winter sky.

Are they trapped in their destiny, or set free also, freed from their past or the need to see me, or the love that bound them to me? Who gains, who loses? The eternal and newly-minted question.

The dog's great feet propel it in long leaps across the shining clearing. When I follow, my feet sink into the snow and I sink into a moonlight struggle with my breath. I am older than I want to be and my body tells me at times like these: remember when you were at the beginning, exploding across every new challenge like this young dog?

The dog has crossed to the willows beyond the broken down fence, and is nosing at a deeper shadow beneath the bushes, then leaping back to me with a happy bark: look what I've found!

Is it a child? No, a teenager, huddled back in a down-filled parka, face inside the hood, a smudge broken by the glint of moonlight on eyes and white teeth. A dark face. Hands bare, pulled from pockets to push away the dog's friendly face. Afraid? Yes.

'Back off, dog!' Reluctantly, wagging half its body, the dog retreats a few yards.

'The dog won't hurt you.' I reach out my hand. 'Neither will I. Would you like to come out of the bushes?'

Silently the youngster takes my hand to pull upright, then lets go and manages without moving to retreat to the furthest corner of the field, the night, the sky.

'Are you cold?'

The muffled head nods. The fur on the coat (fur?) now shades the face completely.

'I have tea at my house. Are you hungry?'

Another nod. Whence sprang this silent apparition? Child of the willows. I laugh, the kid is startled.

'Don't tremble like that,' I say, irritated, 'it makes me nervous. Where did you come from?'

Hand out of pocket to point west, wave across the whole quadrant of sky and scrub prairie. Fine.

'Can you talk?' Only another nod. 'Why don't you, then?' The shoulders rise in a bulky, expressive shrug. Ridiculous conversation. I whistle for the dog, who has found a chunk of wood under a bush, is standing flirtatiously attentive with the stick in its mouth, ears alert.

'Might as well get used to the dog. It lives here with me. It's my friend now, it keeps me company.'

Small guttural voice. 'What's its name?'

'Just the black dog. When it's the only dog around, I don't see the need for a name.'

Silence. The sound of snow and frozen grasses crunching under well-wrapped feet. Mine are boots. The kid has – leather? Moccasins? Must have come from a far distant west, somewhere beyond even my line of night vision.

'You got a name?'

Good question. By the argument I've applied to the dog, I have no name but the fact of my being. The footsteps I make in the snow were until half an hour ago the only human footsteps; we are following my solitary trail through the birch and poplar and pine, past the stream which beneath ice still offers a muffled susurrus. The single footprints don't define me any more.

'Not any more. Call me what you want.'

'Okay.' But that's all.

'And you? Willow child?'

'Call me what you want.' With a brief hand gesture, the youngster turns to the path.

The circle completed with such abrupt, natural grace. A shadow, I walk through, reflexively looking up to see a skiff of cloud, rainbow-edged and insubstantial, blow across the moon. Orion is brightly walking above the fields, warming my face with his archaic splendour. The youngster is oblivious to the sky. If whatever people lived in the west have gone to the stars as my people have gone, this young one has no tendency to watch their tracks, or maybe avoids now the dangerous heavens.

At the cabin where the dog and I live, we humans stamp snow from our feet and shuck off outer skins. The youngster stands out of the parka as a wiry, slender girl, brown-skinned, black hair roughly hacked short and rumpled around a closed, smooth face. Prove it to me, her glance says as from her stance as near the double door as possible she studies my home.

'Do you know where you are going?'

'No.'

'Do you want to stay here?'

Shrug. The beginning of this relationship is as tough as chewing twigs. Never mind. The dog isn't verbal either. It slouches with a clicking of claws to its rag mat in front of the heater, drops the piece of wood it has carried all the way home, falls into a heap with a great oof of breath. The girl laughs at the oofish sigh, sees me see her face opening in a smile, turns away slowly with the smile fading.

'I've forgotten how to talk,' she says. 'Everybody is gone where I come from.'

'Here, too.'

'If I stay here, what?'

'Whatever you want. There's a place for you if you want it. There's plenty of food for three.'

'Okay.'

The shyness between us is washed over with the picayunish of providing blankets, pillows, towels, the spare bed, information about chores, hints, tiny shared pieces of personality. Inside the log-built cabin is like inside the day-domed sky; full of detail and lost to the music and the brilliance of space, stars and night. Even though I have kept things as simple as I can. I look at my hands, which have lost the roughness of country childhood and the smoothness of city youth, have settled down to accumulate wrinkles, scars and experience. The flickering lamp light catches the face of the youngster, projects an unreliable shadow, makes her face older/younger/older in its variable illumination.

'How old are you?' I ask, and she turns until she faces me out of the shadows, her black eyes shadows themselves, and smiles directly at me. 'I'm growing up,' she says, and her cheek dimples. She takes my hand in her brown hands, draws me to the table where the lamp sits, holds my hands and hers into the light. Hers are roughened by cold and work, long-fingered, with knotted joints. Mine are square capable hands, well formed it's true but not as long as hers. She puts her palm to mine to show how my palm is wider. She twines her fingers among mine.

'You don't know,' she says, 'how fast this world here is going around. I get dizzy just trying to stay on.'

'You didn't have to.'

'You didn't either, but you and that dog stayed.'

'Well, it seemed like a good idea at the time.'

She shrugs, untangles her hand, walks to the curtain door of now her room. Stops with the cotton barricade that passes for a door held half aside, in shadow, her face the same dark mystery I saw among the willows.

'It always does – then,' she says, and the curtain falls flat behind her. The dog walks to the curtain, noses around it, stands with hindquarters in this room like half a dog, backs away, comes back to flop beside me, wide chin on my foot.

'That's right,' I say, but not sure if I've talked to the dog, the willow girl, the stars or my own uncertain self, bereft of stars in this many-celled shelter (house/body).

And dreams, and day, and dusk, and night. I am learning how to be dizzy at the speed of consciousness. The speed of light, of synaptic response, of space flight, of the earth's rotation. Why couldn't we use this rapidly whirling sphere like a catapult to hurl us toward expanded consciousness?

We've stayed plastered to its surface like desperate lichens, clinging to the rock that has been our only home.

Even if we can learn to be dizzy, it's one step. Toward the same goal sought by those others who swift away from us at damn near the speed of light, those fickle and far-sighted travellers.

And for them their journey is no more than a physical catapulting, taking their weak and limited bodies inside shells of metal and polymer and hurling them frail into the mystery. Still the same bodies, still the same human bickering about the way to proceed.

For the first time I realize relief, how glad I am to have heard that bickering fade away beyond the earth's ability to hear. How glad I am that silence has fallen again on the night world.

To celebrate my relief, I've welcomed more noise into my silent house? Well, that's a little too romantic a description – the dog's unsophisticated breathing echoes from the walls, and I bustle through the activities of daily living, with all the clatter they entail. And when I sit and am silent, even if the dog is outside, I can hear my own body ticking away, blood's hushed flow through the vessels (like sound of the stream flowing under ice), heart's stubborn throb, click of joints and creak of muscles. I make a lot of noise all by myself.

II

My thoughts fall back to that night when I put out my hand to her (as she cowered under a bush hiding from the black dog) and she took it, took my hand and all I offered with it.

Then she was afraid of the dog, now she rough-houses with it under the dapple shade of leafy spring trees. She has the affinity for shadow which she has always had. Her face has grown thinner and more defined, has lost the puffiness of childhood.

Out among the stars, the people of Earth are travelling.

Here in a small country made of our perceptions, we too are travelling among stars. Though it is now day and the stars are invisible, all of us know they are there. Black dog, brown human (still willow-graceful though her face is welcoming the lines of age), and me.

III

So easy to die inside without ever again seeing the night. Wasn't what I chose a way of dying inside? To stay inside the well of gravity, as it is called, to stay beneath the blanket of air, to limit my life to this generation, no continuity, no connection? These are the tired doubts which come back to trouble me as I sit before the safe and comfortable heater, warming my aching body against the constant changeable moods of age.

Or of humanity. I am no different than I was before the ships left, except that for years I have had fewer people to talk with, to surround me. If it wasn't the odyssey I had to doubt about, it would be some other preoccupation robbing me of the serenity I thought to have earned by now. What's getting old for, if not to settle doubts?

Restless, I shrug into my coat and slide my feet into pile-lined boots, wade through the sticky snow of a chinook wind until I am among the trees, the cabin behind me. The willow woman catches up to me and walks beside me through the night, her hood back and her hair blowing behind her. She does not have to say anything, but occasionally our eyes meet. We have become friends, though it took some time for her to trust me with her not-unusual history of decision and loss. I have found in myself a temptation to talk too much. She smiles and listens, but in her turn she too can tell long stories from her own and other lives and mythologies. She tells them in formal, patterned sentences, which like the orderly beading on her winter moccasins are from the tradition to which she was born and from which she has come a long, long distance.

She helps me across the stream unselfconsciously, such a change from the teenaged child who trembled as I hauled her out from among bushes in mid-winter. Yet for all her words, and smiles, and stories, to me she is still the mysterious country in the west.

At the fence we sit on a fallen log and watch the sky. Orion, skywalker, is low though the night is young. By now I hardly remember to wonder what the other starwalkers are doing. I put out my hands and one at a time she takes them and warms them between hers. My hands are stiffening with arthritic ache, one of the remembered signs of spring.

Time is a ponderous mysterious engine. I cannot imagine how to think properly of it – as a force, a wonder, an absolute? The night's progress to the final night without change or comprehension of how we live like insects clinging to the inexorable path, the blade of grass or flower stem or pine branch that is our immutable span of existence.

The dog has lost the playfulness of puppyhood, comes like a shadow through the midnight to lie down beside me with its massive head against my thigh. I am growing tired, and the willow woman (I still think of her that way, though long since we traded our social, daylight names) pulls me up and indicates the homeward path.

'You go,' I say, and in the full moonlight see her face, with the lined signatures of laughter and the rest of the score life composes. Her face I have always thought was beautiful and mysterious but in the moonlight it seems to open to me like night itself opens out into infinity.

'You always want to be alone with it,' she says.

'It isn't that,' I say. 'But how can I remember the lost human race and be lonely when you're distracting me here?'

She grins. 'Manufacture of melancholy?' But she walks back into the forest and I hear her leap across the stream.

The black dog looks after her, but chooses me, turns again and settles with that rush of spent breath. It can change and grow old, and still be the same through all its changes. And from within I can see myself in the same pattern, learning slowly and living so fast along the time line.

The days, the seasons seem to go by so quickly now. As if now that Earth is almost deserted, there is no drag, no friction of billions to hold it from spinning.

IV

After all, the sky is full of something, be it refracted light of day or direct and uncomplicated starlight. Only the stars themselves are uncomplicated, I mean, for we make so much of them, running after them like the most opaque of lovers, or most of us did –

Except the few stubborn ones who wouldn't play sycophant to the universe. I'm sorry, the naked sky will have to get along without me; I like mine cluttered with atmosphere and obscured with diurnal rhythms.

Oh, what does it matter? Here at the place where I buried the old black dog when it finally loosed its tenacious hold on the years – that's how long ago I came across a snowy field and found the one other human in my part of the world, hiding in the willows, in the snow-field, in the middle of a brilliant night.

Nothing is different. That's the curse of the ones left behind, but also the blessing. They'll see light bend in that Einsteinian grace, they'll see something new every time the ship rolls. The stars will truly wheel and dance, new patterns, new myths and fantasies. We will live something like we always did, or always wanted to, but more solitary.

If loneliness was my concern, why couldn't I go with them? Not just that I was too set in my ways to want that much change, for I knew my life would never be the same whatever I decided. No, I think I was too much in love with the night of the world. Not the pure vacuum-packed darkness of the void, but the lovely imperfect blue-black of Earth, the wavering stars' light bursting through like a revelation of mortality.

And the other one? She was in love with the Earth itself. Its sweet spinning was fast enough for her. She wanted to watch the moon come up forever over the playground of rabbits and wolverines and bears and bright water. She loved the way the contents of the earth roiled and moiled around her. She wouldn't give that up for relentless foraging through a vacuum. So here she is.

That's the matter with some of us. We can't exist in a vacuum. Aware of gravity, we stand spellbound before the stars, but we don't want to get any closer. We love another force, the one that holds us together, to each other, to the ground.

Don't ask me to name that force, I was unable even to give a name to the black dog, nor can I now remember that of the woman who is sharing my old years. They exist, that is all. I have no name myself, I have only got the place where I am. It has been enough.

In the end, like the black dog, we will dissolve into gravity, we will dream dark earth dreams or dream no more.

(Learning About) Machine Sex

A naked woman working at a computer. Which attracts you most? It was a measure of Whitman that, as he entered the room, his eyes went first to the unfolded machine gleaming small and awkward in the light of the long-armed desk lamp; he'd seen the woman before.

Angel was the woman. Thin and pale-skinned, with dark nipples and black pubic hair, and her face hidden by a dark unkempt mane of long hair as she leaned over her work.

A woman complete with her work. It was a measure of Angel that she never acted naked, even when she was. Perhaps especially when she was.

So she has a new board, thought Whitman, and felt his guts stir the way they stirred when he first contemplated taking her to bed. That was a long time ago. And she knew it, felt without turning her head the desire, and behind the screen of her straight dark hair, uncombed and tumbled in front of her eyes, she smiled her anger down.

'Where have you been?' he asked, and she shook her hair back, leaned backward to ease her tense neck.

'What is that thing?' he went on insistently, and Angel turned her face to him, half-scowling. The board on the desk had thin irregular wings spreading from a small central module. Her fingers didn't slow their keyboard dance.

'None of your business,' she said.

She saved the input, and he watched her fold the board into a smaller and smaller rectangle. Finally she shook her hair back from her face.

'I've got the option on your bioware,' he said.

'Pay as you go,' she said. 'New house rule.'

And found herself on her ass on the floor from his reflexive, furious blow. And his hand in her hair, pulling her up and against the wall. Hard. Astonishing her with how quickly she could hurt how much. Then she hurt too much to analyse it.

'You are a bitch,' he said.

'So what?' she said. 'When I was nicer, you were still an asshole.'

Her head back against the wall, crack. Ouch.

Breathless, Angel: 'Once more and you never see this bioware.' And Whitman slowly draws breath, draws back, and looks at her the way she knew he always felt.

'Get out,' she said. 'I'll bring it to Kozyk's office when it's ready.'

So he went. She slumped back in the chair, and tears began to blur her vision, but hate cleared them up fast enough, as she unfolded the board again, so that despite the pain she hardly missed a moment of programming time.

Assault only a distraction now, betrayal only a detail: Angel was on a roll. She had her revenge well in hand, though it took a subtle mind to recognise it.

Again: 'I have the option on any of your bioware.' This time, in the office, Whitman wore the nostalgic denims he now affected, and Angel her street-silks and leather.

'This is mine, but I made one for you.' She pulled it out of the bag. Where her board looked jerry-built, this one was sleek. Her board looked interesting; this one packaged. 'I made it before you sold our company,' she said. 'I put my best into it. You may as well have it. I suppose you own the option anyway, eh?'

She stood. Whitman was unconsciously restless before her.

'When you pay me for this,' she said, 'make it in MannComp stock.' She tossed him the board. 'But be careful. If you take it apart wrong, you'll break it. Then you'll have to ask me to fix it, and from now on, my tech rate goes up.'

As she walked by him, he reached for her, hooked one arm around her waist. She looked at him, totally expressionless. 'Max,' she said, 'it's like I told you last night. From now on, if you want it, you pay. Just like everyone else.' He let her go. She pulled the soft dirty white silk shirt on over the black leather jacket. The compleat rebel now.

'It's a little going away present. When you're a big shot in MannComp, remember that I made it. And that you couldn't even take it apart right. I guarantee.'

He wasn't going to watch her leave. He was already studying the board. Hardly listening, either.

'Call it the Mannboard,' she said. 'It gets big if you stroke it.' She shut the door quietly behind herself.

It would be easier if this were a story about sex, or about machines. It is true that the subject is Angel, a woman who builds computers like they have never been built before outside the human skull. Angel, like everyone else, comes from somewhere and goes somewhere else. She lives in that linear and binary universe. However, like everyone else, she lives concurrently in another universe less simple. Trivalent, quadrivalent, multivalent. World without end, with no amen. And so, on.

They say a hacker's burned out before he's twenty-one. Note the pronoun: he. Not many young women in that heady realm of the chip.

Before Angel was twenty-one – long before – she had taken the cybernetic chip out of a Wm Kuhns fantasy and patented it; she had written the program for the self-taught AI the Bronfmanns had bought and used to gain world prominence for their MannComp lapboard; somewhere in there, she'd lost innocence, and when her clever additions to that AI turned it into something the military wanted, she dropped out of sight in Toronto and went back to Rocky Mountain House, Alberta on a Greyhound bus.

It was while she was thinking about something else – cash, and how to get some – that she had looked out of the bus window in Winnipeg into the display window of a sex shop. Garter belts, sleazy magazines on cheap coated paper with dayglo orange stickers over the genitals of bored sex kings and queens, a variety of ornamental vibrators. She had too many memories of Max to take it lightly, though she heard the laughter of the roughnecks in the back of the bus as they topped each others' dirty jokes, and thought perhaps their humour was worth emulating. If only she could.

She passed her twentieth birthday in a hotel in Regina, where she stopped to take a shower and tap into the phone lines, checking for pursuit. Armed with the money she got through automatic transfer from a dummy account in Medicine Hat, she rode the bus the rest of the way ignoring the rolling of beer bottles under the seats, the acrid stink of the onboard toilet. She was thinking about sex.

As the bus roared across the long flat prairie she kept one hand on the roll of bills in her pocket, but with the other she made the first notes on the program that would eventually make her famous.

She made the notes on an antique NEC lapboard which had been her aunt's, in old-fashioned BASIC – all the machine would support – but she unravelled it and knitted it into that artificial trivalent language when she got to the place at Rocky and plugged the idea into her Mannboard. She had it written in a little over four hours on-time, but that counted an hour and a half she took to write a new loop into the AI. (She would patent that loop later the same year and put the royalties into a blind trust for her brother, Brian, brain damaged from birth. He was in Michener Centre in Red Deer, not educable; no one at Bronfmann knew about her family, and she kept it that way.)

She called it Machine Sex; working title.

Working title for a life: born in Innisfail General Hospital, father a rodeo cowboy who raised rodeo horses, did enough mixed farming out near Caroline to build his young second wife a big log house facing the mountain view. The first baby came within a year, ending her mother's tenure as teller at the local bank. Her aunt was a programmer for the University of Lethbridge, chemical molecular model analysis on the University of Calgary mainframe through a modem link.

From her aunt she learned BASIC, Pascal, COBOL and C; in school she played the usual turtle games on the Apple IIe; when she was fourteen she took a bus to Toronto, changed her name to Angel, affected a punk hairstyle and the insolent all-white costume of that year's youth, and eventually walked into Northern Systems, the company struggling most successfully with bionics at the time, with the perfected biochip, grinning at the proper young men in their grey three-piece suits as they tried to find a bug in it anywhere. For the first million she let them open it up; for the next five she told them how she did it. Eighteen years old by the phoney records she'd cooked on her arrival in Toronto, she was free to negotiate her own contracts.

But no one got her away from Northern until Bronfmann bought Northern lock, stock and climate-controlled work-shop. She had been sleeping with Northern's boy-wonder president by then for about a year, had yet to have an orgasm though she'd learned a lot about kinky sex toys. Figured she'd been screwed by him for the last time when he sold the company without telling her; spent the next two weeks doing a lot of drugs and having a lot of cheap sex in the degenerate punk underground; came up with the AI education program.

Came up indeed, came swaggering into Ted Kozyk's office, president of Bronfmann's MannComp subsidiary, with that jury-rigged Mannboard tied into two black-box add-ons no bigger than a bar of soap, and said, 'Watch this.'

Took out the power supply first, wiped the memory, plugged into a wall outlet and turned it on.

The bootstrap greeting sounded a lot like Goo.

'Okay,' she said, 'it's ready.'

'Ready for what?'

'Anything you want,' she said. By then he knew her, knew her rep, knew that the sweaty-smelling, disheveled, anorectic-looking waif in the filthy, oversized silk shirt (the rebels had affected natural fabrics the year she left home, and she always did after that, even later when the silk was cleaner, more upmarket, and black instead of white) had something. Two weeks ago he'd bought a company on the strength of that something, and the board Whitman had brought him the day after the sale, even without the software to run on it, had been enough to convince him he'd been right.

He sat down to work, and hours later he was playing Go with an AI he'd taught to talk back, play games, and predict horse races and the stock market.

He sat back, flicked the power switch and pulled the plug, and stared at her.

'Congratulations,' she said.

'What for?' he said; 'you're the genius.'

'No, congratulations, you just murdered your first baby,' she said, and plugged it back in. 'Want to try for two?'

'Goo,' said the deck. 'Dada.'

It was her little joke. It was never a feature on the MannComp A-One they sold across every MannComp counter in the world.

But now she's all grown up, she's sitting in a log house near Rocky Mountain house, watching the late summer sunset from the big front windows, while the computer runs Machine Sex to its logical conclusion, orgasm.

She had her first orgasm at nineteen. According to her false identity, she was twenty-three. Her lover was a delegate to MannComp's annual sales convention; she picked him up after the speech she gave on the ethics of selling AIs to high school students in Thailand. Or whatever, she didn't care. Kozyk used to write her speeches but she usually changed them to suit her mood. This night she'd been circumspect, only a few expletives, enough to amuse the younger sales representatives and reassure the older ones.

The one she chose was smooth in his approach and she thought, well, we'll see. They went up to the suite MannComp provided, all mod cons and king-size bed, and as she undressed she looked at him and thought, he's ambitious, this boy, better not give him an inch.

He surprised her in bed. Ambitious maybe, but he paid a lot of attention to detail.

After he spread her across the universe in a way she had never felt before, he turned to her and said, 'That was pretty good, eh, baby?' and smiled a smooth little grin. 'Sure,' she said, 'it was okay,' and was glad she hadn't said more while she was out in the ozone.

By then she thought she was over what Whitman had

done to her. And after all, it had been simple enough, what he did. Back in that loft she had in Hull, upstairs of a shop, where she covered the windows with opaque mylar and worked night and day in that twilight. That night as she worked he stood behind her, hands on her shoulders, massaging her into further tenseness.

'Hey, Max, you know I don't like it when people look over my shoulder when I'm working.'

'Sorry, baby.' He moved away, and she felt her shoulders relax just to have his hands fall away.

'Come on to bed,' he said. 'You know you can pick that up whenever.'

She had to admit he was being pleasant tonight. Maybe he too was tired of the constant scrapping, disguised as jokes, that wore at her nerves so much. All his efforts to make her stop working, slow her down so he could stay up. The sharp edges that couldn't be disguised. Her bravado made her answer in the same vein, but in the mornings, when he was gone to Northern; she paced and muttered to herself, reworking the previous day until it was done with, enough that she could go on. And after all what was missing? She had no idea how to debug it.

Tonight he'd even made some dinner, and touched her kindly. Should she be grateful? Maybe the conversations, such as they were, where she tried to work it out, had just made it worse –

'Ah, shit,' she said, and pushed the board away. 'You're right, I'm too tired for this. *Demain*.' She was learning French in her spare time.

He began with hugging her, and stroking the long line along her back, something he knew she liked, like a cat likes it, arches its back at the end of the stroke. He knew she got turned on by it. And she did. When they had sex at her house he was without the paraphernalia he preferred, but he seemed to manage, buoyed up by some mood she couldn't share; nor could she share his release.

Afterward, she lay beside him, tense and dissatisfied in

the big bed, not admitting it, or she'd have to admit she
didn't know what would help. He seemed to be okay, stretched, relaxed and smiling.

'Had a big day,' he said.

'Yeah?'

'Big deal went through.'

'Yeah?'

'Yeah, I sold the company.'

'You what?' Reflexively moving herself so that none of
her body touched his.

'Northern. I put it to Bronfmann. Megabucks.'

'Are you joking?' but she saw he was not. 'You didn't, I
didn't . . . Northern's *our* company.'

'My company. I started it.'

'I made it big for you.'

'Oh, and I paid you well for every bit of that.'

She got up. He was smiling a little, trying on the little-
boy grin. No, baby, she thought, not tonight.

'Well,' she said, 'I know for sure that this is my bed. Get
out of it.'

'Now, I knew you might take this badly. But it really was
the best thing. The R&D costs were killing us. Bronfmann
can eat them for breakfast.'

R&D costs meant her. 'Maybe. Your clothes are here.'
She tossed them on the bed, went into the other room.

As well as sex, she hadn't figured out betrayal yet either;
on the street, she thought, people fucked you over openly,
not in secret.

This, even as she said it to herself, she recognised as
romantic and certainly not based on experience. She was
street-wise in every way but one: Max had been her first
lover.

She unfolded the new board. It had taken her some time
to figure out how to make it expand like that, to fit the
program it was going to run. This idea of shaping the hardware to the software had been with her since she made the
biochip, and thus made it possible and much more interest-

ing than the other way around. But making the hardware to fit her new idea had involved a great deal of study and technique, and so far she had had limited success.

This reminded her again of sex, and, she supposed, relationships, although it seemed to her that before sex everything had been on surfaces, very easy. Now she had sex, she had had Max, and now she had no way to realize the results of any of that. Especially now, when Northern had just vanished into Bronfmann's computer empire, putting her in the position again of having to prove herself. What had Max used to make Bronfmann take the bait? She knew very clearly: Angel, the Northern Angel, would now become the MannComp Angel. The rest of the bait would have been the AI; she was making more of it every day, but couldn't yet bring it together. Could it be done at all? Bronfmann had paid high for an affirmative answer.

Certainly this time the bioware was working together. She began to smile a little to herself, almost unaware of it, as she saw how she could interconnect the loops to make a solid net to support the program's full and growing weight. Because, of course, it would have to learn as it went along – that was basic.

Angel as metaphor; she had to laugh at herself when she woke from programming hours later, Max still sleeping in her bed, ignoring her eviction notice. He'll have to get up to piss anyway, she thought; that's when I'll get him out. She went herself to the bathroom in the half-dawn light, stretching her cramped back muscles and thinking remotely, well, I got some satisfaction out of last night after all: the beginnings of the idea that might break this impasse. While it's still inside my head, this one is mine. How can I keep it that way?

New fiscal controls, she thought grimly. New contracts, now that Northern doesn't exist any more. Max can't have this, whatever it turns into, for my dowry to MannComp.

When she put on her white silks – leather jacket underneath, against the skin as street fashion would have it – she hardly knew herself what she would do. The little board went into her bag with the boxes of pills the pharmaceutical tailor had made for her. If there was nothing there to suit, she'd buy something new. In the end, she left Max sleeping in her bed; so what? she thought as she reached the highway. The first ride she hitched took her to Toronto, not without a little tariff, but she no longer gave a damn about any of that.

By then the drugs in her system had lifted her out of a body that could be betrayed, and she didn't return to it for two weeks, two weeks of floating in a soup of disjointed noise, and always the program running, unfolding, running again, unfolding inside her relentless mind. She kept it running to drown anything she might remember about trust or the dream of happiness.

When she came home two weeks later, on a hot day in summer with the Ottawa Valley humidity unbearable and her body tired, sore and bruised, and very dirty, she stepped out of her filthy silks in a room messy with Whitman's continued inhabitation; furious, she popped a system cleanser and unfolded the board on her desk. When he came back in she was there, naked, angry, working.

A naked woman working at a computer. What good were cover-ups? Watching Max after she took the new AI up to Kozyk, she was only triumphant because she'd done something Max could never do, however much he might be able to sell her out. Watching them fit it to the bioboard, the strange unfolding machine she had made to fit the ideas only she could have, she began to be afraid. The system cleanser she'd taken made the clarity inescapable. Over the next few months, as she kept adding clever loops and twists, she watched their glee and she looked at what telephone numbers were in the top ten on their modem memories and she began to realize that it was not only business and science that would pay high for a truly thinking machine.

She knew that ten years before there had been Pentagon programmers working to model predatory behaviour in AIs using Prolog and its like. That was old hat. None of them, however, knew what they needed to know to write for her bioware yet. No one but Angel could do that. So, by the end of her nineteenth year, that made Angel one of the most sought-after, endangered ex-anorectics on the block.

She went to conferences and talked about the ethics of selling AIs to teenagers in Nepal. Or something. And took a smooth salesman to bed, and thought all the time about when they were going to make their approach. It would be Whitman again, not Kozyk, she thought; Ted wouldn't get his hands dirty, while Max was born with grime under his nails.

She thought also about metaphors. How, even in the new street slang which she could speak as easily as her native tongue, being screwed, knocked, fucked over, jossed, dragged all meant the same thing: hurt to the core. And this was what people sought out, what they spent their time seeking in pick-up joints, to the beat of bad old headbanger bands, that nostalgia shit. Now, as well as the biochip, Max, the AI breakthrough, and all the tailored drugs she could eat, she'd had orgasm too.

Well, she supposed it passed the time.

What interested her intellectually about orgasm was not the lovely illusion of transcendence it brought, but the absolute binary predictability of it. When you learn what to do to the nerve endings, and they are in a receptive state, the program runs like kismet. Warm boot. She'd known a hacker once who'd altered his bootstrap messages to read 'Warm pussy'. She knew where most hackers were at; they played with their computers more than they played with themselves. She was the same, otherwise why would it have taken a pretty-boy salesman in a three-piece to show her the simple answer? All the others, just like trying to use an old MS-DOS disc to boot up one of her Mann lapboards with crystal RO/RAM.

Angel forgets she's only twenty. Genius is uneven. There's no substitute for time, that relentless shaper of understanding. Etc. Etc. Angel paces with the knowledge that everything is a phase, even this. Life is hard and then you die, and so on. And so, on.

One day it occurred to her that she could simply run away.

This should have seemed elementary but to Angel it was a revelation. She spent her life fatalistically; her only successful escape had been from the people she loved. Her lovely, crazy grandfather; her generous and slightly avaricious aunt; and her beloved imbecile brother: they were buried deep in a carefully forgotten past. But she kept coming back to Whitman, to Kozyk and Bronfmann, as if she liked them.

As if, like a shocked dog in a learned helplessness experiment, she could not believe that the cage had a door, and the door was open.

She went out the door. For old times' sake, it was the bus she chose; the steamy chill of an air-conditioned Greyhound hadn't changed at all. Bottles – pop and beer – rolling under the seats and the stench of chemicals filling the air whenever someone sneaked down to smoke a cigarette or a reef in the toilet. Did anyone ever use it to piss in? She liked the triple seat near the back, but the combined smells forced her to the front, behind the driver, where she was joined, across the country, by an endless succession of old women, immaculate in their fortrels, who started conversations and shared peppermints and gum.

She didn't get stoned once.

The country unrolled strangely: sex shop in Winnipeg, bank machine in Regina, and hours of programming alternating with polite responses to the old women, until eventually she arrived, creased and exhausted, in Rocky Mountain House.

Rocky Mountain House: a comfortable model of a small town, from which no self-respecting hacker should originate. But these days, the world a net of wire and wireless, it doesn't matter where you are, as long as you have the information people want. Luckily for Angel's secret past, however, this was not a place she would be expected to live – or to go – or to come from.

An atavism she hadn't controlled had brought her this far. A rented car took her the rest of the way to the ranch. She thought only to look around, but when she found the tenants packing for a month's holiday, she couldn't resist the opportunity. She carried her leather satchel into their crocheted, frilled guest room – it had been her room fifteen years before – with a remote kind of satisfaction.

That night, she slept like the dead – except for some dreams. But there was nothing she could do about them.

Lightning and thunder. I should stop now, she thought, wary of power surges through the new board which she was charging as she worked. She saved her file, unplugged the power, stood, stretched, and walked to the window to look at the mountains.

The storm illuminated the closer slopes erratically, the rain hid the distances. She felt some heaviness lift. The cool wind through the window refreshed her. She heard the program stop, and turned off the machine. Sliding out the backup capsule, she smiled her angry smile unconsciously. When I get back to the Ottawa Valley, she thought, where weather never comes from the west like it's supposed to, I'll make those fuckers eat this.

Out in the corrals where the tenants kept their rodeo horses, there was animal noise, and she turned off the light to go and look out the side window. A young man was leaning his weight against the reins-length pull of a rearing, terrified horse. Angel watched as flashes of lightning strobed the hackneyed scene. This was where she came from. She remembered her father in the same struggle. And her mother at this window with her, both of them watching the man. Her mother's anger she never understood until now. Her father's abandonment of all that was in the house, including her brother, Brian, inert and restless in his over-sized crib.

Angel walked back through the house, furnished now in the kitschy western style of every trailer and bungalow in this countryside. She was lucky to stay, invited on a generous impulse, while all but their son were away. She felt vaguely guilty at her implicit criticism.

Angel invited the young rancher into the house only because this is what her mother and her grandmother would have done. Even Angel's great-grandmother, whose father kept the stopping house, which meant she kept the travellers fed, even her spirit infused in Angel the unwilling act. She watched him almost sullenly as he left his rain gear in the wide porch.

He was big, sitting in the big farm kitchen. His hair was wet, and he swore almost as much as she did. He told her how he had put a trailer on the north forty, and lived there now, instead of in the little room where she'd been invited to sleep. He told her about the stock he'd accumulated riding the rodeo. They drank Glenfiddich. She told him her father had been a rodeo cowboy. He told her about his university degree in agriculture. She told him she'd never been to university. They drank more whiskey and he told her he couldn't drink that other rot gut any more since he tasted real Scotch. He invited her to see his computer. She went with him across the yard and through the trees in the rain, her bag over her shoulder, board hidden in it, and he showed her his computer. It turned out to be the first machine she designed for Northern – archaic now, compared with the one she'd just invented.

Fair is fair, she thought drunkenly, and she pulled out her board and unfolded it.

'You showed me yours, I'll show you mine,' she said.

He liked the board. He was amazed that she had made it. They finished the Scotch.

'I like you,' she said. 'Let me show you something. You can be the first.' And she ran Machine Sex for him.

He was the first to see it: before Whitman and Kozyk who bought it to sell to people who already have had and done everything; before David and Jonathan, the Hardware Twins in MannComp's Gulf Islands shop, who made the touchpad devices necessary to run it properly; before a world market hungry for the kind of glossy degradation Machine Sex could give them bought it in droves from a hastily-created – MannComp-subsidiary – numbered company. She ran it for him with just the automouse on her board, and a description of what it would do when the hardware was upgraded to fit.

It was very simple, really. If orgasm was binary, it could be programmed. Feed back the sensation through one or more touchpads to program the body. The other thing she knew about human sex was that it was as much cortical as genital, or more so: touch is optional for the turn-on. Also easy, then, to produce cortical stimuli by programmed input. The rest was a cosmetic elaboration of the premise.

At first it did turn him on, then off, then it made his blood run cold. She was pleased by that: her work had chilled her too.

'You can't market that thing!' he said.

'Why not. It's a fucking good program. Hey, get it? Fucking good.'

'It's not real.'

'Of course it isn't. So what?'

'So, people don't need that kind of stuff to get turned on.'

She told him about people. More people than he'd known were in the world. People who made her those designer drugs, given in return for favours she never granted until after Whitman sold her like a used car. People like Whitman, teaching her about sexual equipment while dealing with the Pentagon and CSIS to sell them Angel's sharp angry mind, as if she'd work on killing others as eagerly as she was trying to kill herself. People who would hire a woman on the street, as they had her during that two-week nightmare almost a year before, and use her as casually as their own hand, without giving a damn.

'One night,' she said, 'just to see, I told all the johns I was fourteen. I was skinny enough, even then, to get away with it. And they all loved it. Every single one gave me a bonus, and took me anyway.'

The whiskey fog was wearing a little thin. More time had passed than she thought, and more had been said than she had intended. She went to her bag, rummaged, but she'd left her drugs in Toronto, some dim idea at the time that she should clean up her act. All that had happened was that she had spent the days so tight with rage that she couldn't eat, and she'd already cured herself of that once; for the record, she thought, she'd rather be stoned.

'Do you have any more booze?' she said, and he went to look. She followed him around his kitchen.

'Furthermore,' she said, 'I rolled every one of them that I could, and all but one had pictures of his kids in his wallet, and all of them were teenagers. Boys and girls together. And their saintly dads out fucking someone who looked just like them. Just like them.'

Luckily, he had another bottle. Not quite the same quality, but she wasn't fussy.

'So I figure,' she finished, 'that they don't care who they

fuck. Why not the computer in the den? Or the office system at lunch hour?'

'It's not like that,' he said. 'It's nothing like that. People deserve better.' He had the neck of the bottle in his big hand, was seriously, carefully pouring himself another shot. He gestured with both bottle and glass. 'People deserve to have – love.'

'Love?'

'Yeah, love. You think I'm stupid, you think I watched too much TV as a kid, but I know it's out there. Somewhere. Other people think so too. Don't you? Didn't you, even if you won't admit it now, fall in love with that guy Max at first? You never said what he did at the beginning, how he talked you into being his lover. Something must have happened. Well, that's what I mean: love.'

'Let me tell you above love. Love is a guy who talks real smooth taking me out to the woods and telling me he just loves my smile. And then taking me home and putting me in leather handcuffs so he can come. And if I hurt he likes it, because he likes it to hurt a little and he thinks I must like it like he does. And if I moan he thinks I'm coming. And if I cry he think it's love. And so do I. Until one evening – not too long after my *last* birthday, as I recall – he tells me that he has sold me to another company. And this only after he fucks me one last time. Even though I don't belong to him any more. After all, he had the option on all my bioware.'

'All that is just politics.' He was sharp, she had to grant him that.

'Politics,' she said, 'give me a break. Was it politics made Max able to sell me with the stock: hardware, software, liveware?'

'I've met guys like that. Women too. You have to understand that it wasn't personal to him, it was just politics.' Also stubborn. 'Sure, you were naïve, but you weren't wrong. You just didn't understand company politics.'

'Oh, sure I did. I always have. Why do you think I

changed my name? Why do you think I dress in natural fibres and go through all the rest of this bullshit? I know how to set up power blocs. Except in mine there is only one party – me. And that's the way it's going to stay. Me against them from now on.'

'It's not always like that. There are assholes in the world, and there are other people too. Everyone around here still remembers your grandfather, even though he's been retired in Camrose for fifteen years. They still talk about the way he and his wife used to waltz at the Legion Hall. What about him? There are more people like him than there are Whitmans.'

'Charlotte doesn't waltz much since her stroke.'

'That's a cheap shot. You can't get away with cheap shots. Speaking of shots, have another.'

'Don't mind if I do. Okay, I give you Eric and Charlotte. But one half-happy ending doesn't balance out the people who go through their lives with their teeth clenched, trying to make it come out the same as a True Romance comic, and always wondering what's missing. They read those bodice-ripper novels, and make that do for the love you believe in so naïvely.' Call her naïve, would he? Two could play at that game. 'That's why they'll all go crazy for Machine Sex. So simple. So linear. So fast. So uncomplicated.'

'You underestimate people's ability to be happy. People are better at loving than you think.'

'You think so? Wait until you have your own little piece of land and some sweetheart takes you out in the trees on a moonlit night and gives you head until you think your heart will break. So you marry her and have some kids. She furnishes the trailer in a five-room sale grouping. You have to quit drinking Glenfiddich because she hates it when you talk too loud. She gets an allowance every month and crochets a cozy for the TV. You work all day out in the rain and all evening in the back room making the books balance on the outdated computer. After the kids come she gains weight and sells real estate if you're lucky. If not she makes things out of recycled bleach bottles and hangs them in the yard. Pretty soon she wears a nightgown to bed and turns her back when you slip in after a hard night at the keyboard. So you take up drinking again and teach the kids about the rodeo. And you find some square-dancing chick who gives you head out behind the bleachers one night in Trochu, so sweet you think your heart will break. What you gonna do then, mountain man?'

'Okay, we can tell stories until the sun comes up. Which won't be too long, look at the time; but no matter how many stories you tell, you can't make me forget about that thing.' He pointed to the computer with loathing.

'It's just a machine.'

'You know what I mean. That thing in it. And besides, I'm gay. Your little scenario wouldn't work.'

She laughed and laughed. 'So that's why you haven't made a pass at me yet.' She wondered coldly how gay he was, but she was tired, so tired of proving power. His virtue was safe with her; so, she thought suddenly, strangely, was hers with him. It was unsettling and comforting at once.

'Maybe,' he said. 'Or maybe I'm just a liar like you think everyone is. Eh? You think everyone strings everyone else a line? Crap. Who has the time for that shit?'

Perhaps they were drinking beer now. Or was it vodka? She found it hard to tell after a while.

'You know what I mean,' she said. 'You should know. The sweet young thing who has AIDS and doesn't tell you. Or me. I'm lucky so far. Are you? Or who sucks you for your money. Or josses you 'cause he's into denim and Nordic looks.'

'Okay, okay. I give up. Everybody's a creep but you and me.'

'And I'm not so sure about you.'

'Likewise, I'm sure. Have another. So, if you're so pure, what about the ethics of it?'

'What *about* the ethics of it?' she asked. 'Do you think I

went through all that sex without paying attention? I had nothing else to do but watch other people come. I saw that old cult movie, where the aliens feed on heroin addiction and orgasm, and the woman's not allowed orgasm so she has to O.D. on smack. Orgasm's more decadent than shooting heroin? I can't buy that, but there's something about a world that sells it over and over again. Sells the thought of pleasure as a commodity, sells the getting of it as if it were the getting of wisdom. And all these times I told you about, I saw other people get it through me. Even when someone finally made me come, it was just a feather in his cap, an accomplishment, nothing personal. Like you said. All I was was a program, they plugged into me and went through the motions and got their result. Nobody cares if the AI finds fulfilment running their damned data analyses. Nobody thinks about depressed and angry Mannboard ROMs. They just think about getting theirs.'

'So why not get mine?' She was pacing now, angry, leaning that thin body as if the wind were against her. 'Let me be the one who runs the program.'

'But you won't be there. You told me how you were going to hide out, all that spy stuff.'

She leaned against the wall, smiling a new smile she thought of as predatory. And maybe it was. 'Oh, yes,' she said. 'I'll be there the first time. When Max and Kozyk run this thing and it turns them on. I'll be there. That's all I care to see.'

He put his big hands on the wall on either side of her and leaned in. He smelled of sweat and liquor and his face was earnest with intoxication.

'I'll tell you something,' he said. 'As long as there's the real thing, it won't sell. They'll never buy it.'

Angel thought so too. Secretly, because she wouldn't give him the satisfaction of agreement, she too thought they would not go that low. *That's right*, she told herself, *trying to sell it is all right – because they will never buy it.*

But they did.

A woman and a computer. Which attracts you most? Now you don't have to choose. Angel has made the choice irrelevant.

In Kozyk's office, he and Max go over the ad campaign. They've already tested the program themselves quite a lot; Angel knows this because it's company gossip, heard over the cubicle walls in the washrooms. The two men are so absorbed that they don't notice her arrival.

'Why is a woman better than a sheep? Because sheep can't cook. Why is a woman better than a Mannboard? Because you haven't bought your sensory add-on.' Max laughs.

'And what's better than a man?' Angel says; they jump slightly. 'Why, your MannComp touchpads, with two-way input. I bet you'll be able to have them personally fitted.'

'Good idea,' says Kozyk, and Whitman makes a note on his lapboard. Angel, still stunned though she's had weeks to get used to this, looks at them, then reaches across the desk and picks up her prototype board. 'This one's mine,' she says. 'You play with yourselves and your touchpads all you want.'

'Well, you wrote it, baby,' said Max. 'If you can't come with your own program . . . '

Kozyk hiccoughs a short laugh before he shakes his head. 'Shut up, Whitman,' he says. 'You're talking to a very rich and famous woman.'

Whitman looks up from the simulations of his advertising storyboards, smiling a little, anticipating his joke. 'Yeah. It's just too bad she finally burned herself out with this one. They always did say it gives you brain damage.'

But Angel hadn't waited for the punch line. She was gone.

'You'll Remember Mercury'

I

You can rely on the computers, you can train
your crew to competence, you can still take an accidental
ellipse around a dark star and come out halfway across the
span of space. You can't take a heart through the distance
between souls without expecting a warp to transform it.
Then the result is not clear, then the understanding must
be passed through the same course, to give it the same
polarization. O, you find this universe a strange place to
live, my foreign and bewildered friend.

II

It is morning, and the ordinary sun is rising on the ordinary
scene. The sharp shadows still lie long on the quiet town,
my quiet room. You lie sprawled where you fell asleep, the
sunlight's edge crossing your face severely, a right angle

threatening your eye. I sit where I have sat the night, in the wooden rocking chair, unchanged except that with the dawn the cat has come to warm my belly with its light sleep. I captured it too, as I capture you, by feeding the organism. What you need? You amaze me by showing it, that I have something with which to feed you.

You stir and reach out for your particular breakfast.

III

Captain Casey became conscious in the padded chair after a long (how long?) time of stunned half-listening to the efforts of the machinery. So the pain that persisted in the inner ears no longer obscured the hearing: it was a first tentative command evaluation. Finally sluggishly she could turn her head to scan the cabin, where she should see the other crew members – reaching for their switches, shaking blood from their ears? But they were all still unconscious and she could not yet raise her hands to the release or to the computer link.

Bart alone stirred and his opening eyes met hers blankly. Slow comprehension turned his head to the screens. The one view she had not scanned, had not wished to until someone else was awake to share the astonishment. The strange stars, and stranger, the long ship. The stranger. *And we like a couple of (yes, astonished) rabbits, wide-eyed watch this new and alien manifestation*, she thought, and activated the computer link.

The quiet voice added to the whispers. Bart was releasing the emergency restraints. How enviable the large flat fingers, their athletic competence intact. Hers were still bandaged, or tender with new scars.

The voice says 'Scan tempo', it says 'Damage report', it says 'Am I directed to start cryonic procedures on damaged crew members?' Implacable. She turned away after her responses, releasing herself to wonder.

The uncontrolled spin of the ship slowed and stabilized and the pressure normalized. Still the cameras on their gyros kept the viewscreen a stable field of disbelief, and the scene did not dissolve into the starmap she expected to see.

The alien vessel was closer, was closing. The hand reaching out for them. She and Bart were the only living beings now on her small misdirected ship.

The data flowed. The slingshot of an elliptical orbit around a star? A descent through some new black hole, hell hole? *How fortunate*, she thought in passing, *that we can represent the species*. But not reproduce it, thinking of her incomplete Fallopian tubes and Bart's spacer sterility.

Methodically she reported, launched the message capsule. She was not overly surprised to see its silver trajectory end in an orifice of the alien ship. She was startled, however, at its immediate reappearance and resumption of previous course.

There are more things in heaven and earth, Horatio, than are dreamt of in your philosophy. Bart was smiling but he could not talk. He had a strange twisted smile now, the scar on his cheek still pink. She began to unwind the bandages from her hand. Their hold was tenacious where the skin was yet too new to be safely exposed, but she had no leisure for healing now.

They stripped to the skin in their noisy silence, pulled overalls from lockers and donned them. She contemplated ordering Bart to clean his lank hair but at the last moment, it seemed, before her words, he followed her lead and dipped his head through the sanitizer. She pulled his hair gently together at the back, tied it with a scrap of tape. They had been in space a long time, she thought. He offered his hands to her hair, but she shook her head and bound it herself. She was still captain.

Finally, the last step of the ritual. She punched the contact sequence out of the computer, sent it out in all modes. When the answer clicked through, the formulae, the square roots, the spectra of an alien sun, they were ready in their pressure suits, ready for whatever form the summons would take.

IV

We are friendly. We are a bipedal, bisexual intelligent life form capable of peace. (Naturally this capability presupposes certain indiscretions in our collective past. We do not mention these at first.)

(We are bewildered.) Please explain yourselves to us. How did we arrive here? We do not know this quadrant. (We are stripped to the skin again; why bother with clean uniforms? We are examined. It is difficult to tell how.) I am Captain Casey of the Scout Ship Emeritus (this formula occurs to me from some nostalgic impulse) and this is my (go for broke, I'll give him a promotion) alter-in-command Nguyen Bart (they won't understand this); we are representatives of Earth, a planet of oxygen-nitrogen atmosphere circling a G-type star. Earth, or Terra as it is more formally known (would you like to buy the Brooklyn Bridge? if it's still there when we get back from wherever the hell we are), is interested in establishing mutually beneficial friendships throughout the galaxy. This is our first contact with non-Terran life. (You are our first lover. Be gentle.)

V

Meanwhile, on Terra, I have sold you the Brooklyn Bridge too, I think: will you find out you are getting a placebo? But you seem to like it.

'You do not understand,' you say gently when you feel that thought. 'You have exactly what I need.' I look at my violin, as far away as Arcturus now, or as your dark star, whichever it may be. The cat is jealous and pushes its head under your hand. You were interested at first but used it up

very quickly. Still, it is what they call a dumb animal and
doesn't know when to retire. I will know, I am sure, when
the time comes.

You are amused by my Brooklyn Bridge analogy. You
tell me the story of how you thought that irrelevant thought
while bravely doing your duty for home and planet. I have
heard the story on numerous video reconstructions, but from
you it sounds new, fresh. I realize foolishly, after the fact,
that it should; you were there first.

VI

After a long time of talking and trying to listen, although
there is little to hear, Casey sensed a change in the audience.
They were alone. Bart was still with her, she was fortunate.
Food was being provided. She had tried to stress the human
need for food and sleep and companionship. The latter had
been an improvisation based on the growing strangeness.
The food was from their ship, and so were the wide pallets.
After a while she and Bart shared one. He still could not
talk, but she was appalled to discover that she now understood anything he wanted to say.

He was supportive through the crisis of identity and belief
(her analytical mind realized such a crisis was bound to
occur) which followed, she held him through his attack of
fear, and eventually inevitably they made love. Throughout,
she kept in mind that she was still nominally the Captain.
Her command status was not under question.

However, this new and alien relationship caused everything else familiar to come into question.

The data their reacting bodies were providing to the aliens
was also a concern. Casey lay, later sat, awake long after
Bart was dreaming. She was dreaming too, but she could
no longer imagine an end to it all.

Bart represented the familiar, but this new conjunction

was infatuating. Was amazing in its differences and similarities.

Later Bart awoke and tried to talk with her, but she was too tired to stay attentive. She gave him his orders – keep watch, make copious notes (on his cuff? she smiled) and do not allow yourself to be taken away from here without awakening me.

She slept.

VII

I am taller than you are. I am always surprised by that, by the way you fit your shoulder under my arm in such a confident way. You don't talk sometimes for hours, then seem startled when I speak. The months in the ship with your silent co-pilot (alter, if you must promote him) has conditioned you to a certain reality.

Even when you were removed from us altogether and changed, we still kept some of you, enough that your hunger is still real.

You laugh at my conceit, and stroke the cat in whom you have taken a new interest.

'You make the mistake,' you say, 'of assuming that because I am not akin to you, I am one of them.'

Everyone else but me is one of a pervasive *them*. You make a mistake, of thinking I need to know which kind you are.

VIII

She dreamed vividly about her career. She had become a spacer very young, run away from home to become a cabin-person, or the modern analogue. Worked her way up through the ranks. Took what she could, but wasn't greedy. Took whomsoever she could, with due attention to keeping her private life separate from her career. Had, briefly, a husband and a wife who bore her a child, but the long absences took their toll on that as on many Air Force (should be Vacuum Force now, she'd always thought) marriages. Had a citation for her part in a successful rescue operation behind Venus (simple, really, except for the publicity).

Bart she had promoted to co-pilot last trip. Field commission, and yesterday (whenever) another in situ promotion, to alter. She had a good crew, now in cryonic suspense, waiting for the outcome of this encounter.

She dreamed, finally, of the alien touch. The contact she had yearned to make, day-dreamed through its predictable script to the rewards on Terra. But now, was making contact with an entity who was not party to her fantasy screenplay. Like the effort required to keep a balance in her marriage, an effort of empathy was required of her. This time she was the sycophant, longing for a touch, for understanding. A role unsettling in its unfamiliarity.

The longing, the touch, awakened her. She had curled in a half circle in her dreaming, one hand at her groin and the other across her face. The odour of the alien was sweet.

Bart was gone.

IX

She was jealous without believing herself. She wanted to be with them, instead of him. It was her place. She stroked the scars on her hands, the burns where the hot metal had annealed a new surface. That was during the first malfunction. The second had catapulted them here. *Have we been off course since the first, to bring us into some mysterious relationship with the power that was strong enough to throw us here, to bring us into this mysterious relationship?*

X

You pick up my violin in your scarred hands, stroke its smooth curved back. In your grasp its shape seems tortured too.

'Why don't you play for me?' you say, looking away from me into the varnished depths.

I am brushing my hair. I know that if I can entice you to look at me, you may forget that I have not answered. I have no answer. You have all my answers, I have nourished you with them, yet you are still hungry.

I believe you tried with Bart, but he speaks a silent tongue, a foreign one. You came back to Earth hungry, and we feed you, the small animal and I.

XI

She came to meet them again, came to learn more of joy than she could hope to teach. It was difficult to understand what was said, or feel what was done. She had to learn to rely on intuition, a difficult lesson. She was seldom able to be with them without Bart's presence, his chatter, his continual questions. He would never speak again, but this was never an impediment to understanding what he had to say.

He apparently did not share her awareness, however, nor her perceptions. Each of them tried explorations of the vessel but each found a different landscape. They had, finally, no basis for dialogue at all. He obeyed her when necessary. She was preoccupied. He explored his own peculiar euphoria. She grew into her own understanding.

She was, they were, returned to their ship and given a course for home. Little attention was paid by their mentors to detail, but they were still able to reach Earth without a serious lapse of health or welfare. Two of the crew in cryonic suspension deteriorated beyond saving, however. She mourned their accelerated deaths.

XII

We are your people. We return with news of a new race (will you race, to meet them?) We are tired from a long journey through uncharted space.

We have come home (what is this room, these questions? What more can I say?) Home is where our hearts are (but ah, my heart, my heart. You are strangers to me now, no one of you less than alien.

(There is no more certainty here, less, than in the alien ship. So many risks we took, to come home, to find what we called home,

(one among the many dark stars.)

XIII

I watch you as I have watched since first I saw you. You sleep now, so I cannot learn anything new about your alien tastes.

You are a lonely woman and so am I. We feed each other with the words, the actions that succour us through the long days.

My violin is in my lap but I cannot yet play. You are too far from me on the long ellipse of night. Your course curves around the dark star of your solitude and you will slingshot back again and again to enter into orbit around the home of your desires.

You have been parsecs further in real space than I, but you cannot lessen the distance between souls, though your heart wants to rest from its journeys.

Time is the School in Which We Learn, Time is the Fire in Which We Burn

Dedicated to the memory of Laura Estock

I don't have much time.

Time is the power that shrivels souls. There is no heart to it – only a relentless running that takes us nowhere.

Play the game play the game. That's what I'm going to do. Pretend there's no harm to it.

But in the middle of the night a voice speaks very clearly saying it's all a lie. I'm not ready to undertake a fiction for the world's sake. What's the world got on me, anyway? But for a few misdemeanors for which I paid royally, the rest of my life's been a kind of blameless plodding, not entirely uninspired but never distinguished.

By anything.

Okay. What's the story? You're right to ask. I'm tired of telling it though. I've been for a ride in the memory machine too often lately; I can hear its clockwork creak and groan now above the sweetest whisper of my past. You live a thing too often and you use it up.

These days even living once seems to be too often for my body; it's almost used up now. Some say you can wish yourself into oblivion but I never cared to try. It always seemed so pointless to go there. But if I have willed myself anywhere it is into this Slough of Despond; I read the Pilgrim's Progress when I was young, in the abridged children's version, but I still remember the name of the Slough and I recognized it when I arrived here again.

Not content with half measures, I brought my body with me. I just woke up to the fear one morning and I've been eating it with my Rice Krispies ever since.

Ever since. Funny pair of words. Since the mutation of cells in my body started a growth I can't stop. Some mysterious power in my DNA. What is it? No answers. There is some mysterious power to cure it too. What is it? 'We don't have all the answers,' says the woman behind the desk. She looks older than I do by far, though we were classmates in high school. She has taken on the weight of more than just my death. She has become Parent to the World. I see it in her weary gentleness, feel it in her kind hands as they examine me. Her hands are cool and dry, like my mother's hands when she would hold my feverish head for me as a child throwing up into a basin. Was that the foreshadowing, that some day this woman with my mother's hands would play mother to my dying, tell me there could still be hope, that medical science doesn't have all the answers?

At home there is a father, but not mine; he is my husband. He takes care of the kids while I wait here for answers. They ask him, 'Daddy, where's Mommy?' and he says, 'She's sleeping in the hospital for a few days,' and they say, 'But why, Daddy? Doesn't she like sleeping with you any more?' and he tells them stories and they too sleep. Then he comes and tells me and we laugh.

You can laugh, or you can cry; so you might as well laugh. Right? But sometimes I want to cry. I want to cry; I want to cry with him. I'm tired of the game of keeping everybody laughing.

He used to be so dear to me my heart turned over thinking

of him. Now he's just another shadow in the world of the living.

I would like to have him back. I'm not sure about the world yet, but I'm certain I want him. He was so good to hold onto.

Okay, world, I'll make you a bargain. If I can have him, and you throw the kids in as a bonus, I'll agree to take you as well. Wholesale. I'll take you complete with the Ayatollah Khomeini and Mu'ammar Kadhafi and Margaret Thatcher and all those contemporary news figures. I'll take the whole package including starvation and unhappiness and human rights abuse. If I can have my old man back for a while, the one I used to love when I could still feel.

And maybe, if I have to take racism and AIDS and El Salvador, maybe I could have my parents back as well. I know it's a hard bargain, but it seems I used to love them too, and there's certainly room in my hollow heart for at least the few people I loved most, if not the whole crew of friends and neighbours and aunts and cousins. Them I can get back on my own, maybe, once I've made a start.

The thing is, what's the point of getting them back if I have to leave, myself, so soon after? It'll be a long journey for them for nothing. The distant place where I have climbed for safety will be hard for them to reach, and how will they get back when I've gone?

I don't know what to think. Give me some time to think about it, world, before we sign the papers. I wouldn't want to do something I'll regret.

Maybe I should just bargain for a little sleep. For once a good night without waking like this to stare at the darkened ceiling and the fan of weak light from the corridor. There are vague noises, people at their work on the night shift. Though they occasionally visit to check on me, they have nothing to do with me. They are for the acutely sick and the dramatically dying. I won't die tonight. They know they don't have to worry about that.

I wish I didn't have to think about them. No, I don't,

better to think about them than keep wondering what's going to happen when I die. Long corridors, beings of light, all that stuff is just the beginning. Will I become in time the child with whom my sister is pregnant? Or maybe I won't be able to go through the same family again. Maybe a short life starving in India. Lord knows I never lacked for food in this life; until the wasting started I was better padded than most. To think I was worried about it! Now my bones stick out all over.

I miss that comfortable layer of fat. It kept me insulated.

Obviously not insulated enough. Or I wouldn't be lying here being eaten from within.

Eaten. 'What's eating on you?' my father used to say. What was eating on me? Maybe the same thing that gnaws at my gut now, but younger and quieter then, as I was. Doesn't help to wonder what would have happened if I had learned some things earlier and had never learned others at all. Who I'd be today. If I'd still be dying.

I don't like this dying. Never mind the philosophical implications – it's the real mess of it I hate. How the tubes feel and how the veins get tough and rude after too many intravenous feedings and how the stomach turns at the taste of barium. It's a sordid business, living, and dying's worse. I've always hated how even a relatively healthy body is always ready to turn on you. Little things that cause undue pain and problems. Menstruation. Haemorrhoids. Dandruff. Cold sores. Winter flu. Every one of them designed for some kind of displeasure. Not to speak of the functions of the healthy body, like farting in public, which one must never do, learn strategies to avoid: the silent fart; the tightened sphincter; the fast trip to another (empty, non-reverberating) room. Never mind. I'm dying of cancer, and preoccupied with the social implications of the fart? Yep. That's the way we humans are. Petty and foolish.

Doesn't do any good being petty and foolish here in the half-dark: I'm just being cute. As if I had an audience. For the audience I still sing and dance. The fat woman still jolly though no longer able to play the role in public. But the doctors and nurses and my poor lonely husband all know who I used to be, though they see a shadow of the laughing woman now. 'You always wanted me to lose weight,' I say jovially to my husband; I use the same line on the doctor the next morning – too good to use only once. Neither of them winces. We will all keep up the pretence.

I can see them all now, ranged around the bed watching me dance. There are rows of dim faces on the other side of the stage, but I'm not ready to cross yet, so I turn and find in the audience my husband, my parents. They aren't laughing, they aren't applauding. As the rest of the audience fades, they stand waiting for me to finish, to make up my mind: my husband patient as always, my father with his fingers tapping, my mother with a book in her hand, interrupted in her curiosity by my performance.

The rings of the curtain whisper as the young nurse brushes it aside to come to the bedside with her small tray. Rest for the wicked, sleep for the damned. I didn't hear her soft footfalls – though come to think of it there was a quiet treading which I took to be the feet of Death. Better luck next time.

'You don't mean that,' she says, and hands me a glass of water to wash down the cupful of pills. Did I speak aloud? I must be careful. Head back down with a sigh; I'm tired even after the slightest of fancy footwork. The pillow seems so hard.

She pulls my covers straight, tweaks a wrinkle out of the undersheet, puts a warm strong arm under my back to hold me up while she plumps the pillow. She has a worried, earnest face like that of a probationer who is trying to do the best possible job.

'I've only been out of training for five months,' she says, 'but I've done enough.'

And, 'There, that's better,' she says. 'Just like Mum used to do it.'

'Thanks,' I say.

'Shhh,' she says. 'You're supposed to be sleeping.'

'Can't sleep,' I say, 'too many visitors waiting.'

'Tell them all to leave you alone until morning.'

'This may be the last time I see them,' I say, conscious of melodrama but no longer caring, and thinking perhaps if I can shock her into a direct gaze, she won't listen to what I'm thinking any more.

'Well, then, tell them to be quiet when they go. People here are sleeping, and if I can hear them all the way out to the desk, they are making too much noise.'

'Can you hear them?'

'Oh, yes. I can hear everyone's. Hush now, and try to rest a little. You've got a busy day tomorrow.'

'I'm used to the tests. It beats the working world.'

'You won't say that when I get you up at six.' She grins and picks up her tray from the bedside stand, brushes out past the curtain, too busy to do more than nod at my husband, who stands silently, somewhat tousled, in his bathrobe.

'I hear you've been making deals,' he says. 'So you want me back?'

'I'm not sure,' I say. 'What if it's only for a week or a month? I have to make some preparations to go, you know. I can't just jump, like off a cliff. It's not easy to die. It takes energy.'

'You know I'd be just as happy if you stay.'

'I know. I have to think it all out. Where are the kids?'

'They're asleep. You know how easy kids sleep, even when they're worried. I can't sleep.'

'You should. You'll be exhausted tomorrow.'

'I keep having dreams . . . '

He comes forward to the bed and sits beside me, dejected, tired, alone. I put a hand on his back, rub it. 'Why didn't you tell me?'

'I thought you had enough to worry about.'

Ah, my sweetheart. I sit up and put my arms around him,

and he turns, and hugs awkwardly, and puts his head on my shoulder, and begins to cry.

'Ah, sweetheart,' I say.

God, how I've wanted to do this, he thinks. And now it's so easy.

Why didn't he trust me before, I think.

'I didn't know you had time,' he says. It's hard to detach oneself after so many years of leaning on each other. I used to lean on him too, and let my tears flow. How I want to do that again, if only I could.

But still, I let him go; I can't cry. Behind my eyes a little stinging feeling, that's all. Because no matter how many tears are shed for me, they are falling into someone else's river. And my own is damn near dry.

My husband goes off to sleep, with a last kiss and a stroke to my hair before he goes.

Three adults are standing in the shadows behind him. They look vaguely familiar, but I can't place them, until one says uncertainly, 'Mom?'

I speak my children's names and see the strangers nod, each in turn, like marionettes. But they are not marionettes, and their faces are suffused with a mix of grief and wonder. And perhaps disbelief.

'I'm not much like you remember me, am I?'

'You were – fatter,' says the young woman. She is very slim, without looking pinched. She always did take after my husband. She looks very smooth in what must be the trendy clothes of her time.

'You look good,' I say.

'Thanks,' she says. 'I wish you could see me now.'

'But I am seeing you.'

'You know. All the time.'

'Does that mean I'm not going to make it?'

'Oh, Mom!' says the oldest, with an inflection I remember. 'Don't you remember?'

'It hasn't happened to me yet,' I say. 'But let's not talk about that. Tell me about yourselves. Are you happy?'

The older man, and the woman, so hard to think they are familiar to me, look good, but the younger man looks tired and wan. If I die, I know he'll miss me.

'Mom,' he says, 'I wish you were here. I need someone to talk with about this.'

'Talk to your father.'

'He's too busy, and I don't think he wants to listen. He's afraid of emotion. He hasn't been the same since you –'

'Look, Mom, the thing is, it's up to you. And the way you're going about it now, we'll end up missing you. Can't you decide to live, for our sakes?' The oldest was always the most demanding. Now he presses me more than I want to be pressed.

'It's not just you,' I say. 'I come into it too.'

'We don't want you to go so early,' says my daughter, looking a lot like me but with her face more honest and earnest. 'But it's up to you. Do what you think is best.'

'Go to sleep now,' I say. 'I'll let you know.' They reach out to me in a great untidy group hug which reminds me of bedtime as it is now, when they are still small. 'I love you, Mom.' 'Me too.' 'I love you.'

'I love you,' I answer, as they fade away.

And though it's true I feel my love for them again, I also feel a wave of anger, they think I can do everything for them, including overturn death. And if it were possible, they think it would be easy. And they think I would want to do it, just because they have asked me.

The river pulls and pulls at me, and I am tired, almost too tired to stand against it, though I am still afraid of where it would take me if I let it. Dizzy with demands, I still cannot rest, what's the way to rest? Is it dying, or living, or giving up the choice altogether? I wish I were not so alone, so very much alone, not knowing how to choose or what the choice means, not knowing what to do but forced to do it by myself.

'Never mind, daughter,' says my mother, cool hands on my forehead. 'That's what comes of being adult. You ride downstream alone.'

'Just so,' says my father, holding my hand as he used to do when I was a child and couldn't sleep.

'Now I go back,' I say.

'No, forward,' he says. 'It just seems retrograde because you're in new territory.'

'Come on, now,' I say, 'isn't that just what I'd like to believe.'

'In this instance,' says my mother, who after fifty years with him has learned to talk like him, 'we act in place of Universal Truth. What we tell you is unquestionably true.'

'And all that jazz,' says Dad, who after fifty years has learned some of her tricks too. Like how she makes her hands warm or cold by biofeedback to give me what I most need. His hands are warm now.

'Only grown-ups cry,' he says, and indeed I can't seem to help crying now. The snows in the high country are melting, the dry river bed is stunned by a fast swelling torrent. My forehead hot with fever, my mother's cool hands smoothing my skin, her calmness, my father's strength, or vice versa, they so busily becoming each other and I my young self, needing to be picked up after falling down. I have fallen. The current washes over me. I cling to solid ground.

'I can't tell you things will be all right,' says their voice.

Their hands fade and I am torn away from the bank, tumbled downstream. Face into the pillow, crying over spilt milk, enough water in it, cry me a river, I could be singing the blues if only I could speak. This is a messy and unappetizing business, this sobbing, this weeping, swept off to another country, leaving only a kernel of mind for a sentry, I felt safe standing on the river bank, now I'm watching myself being swept toward the rapids, the high falls, the edge. Then swept away in the rush of tears, feeling the rocks below give way to space as the brink is crossed, falling falling falling until I splash into the pool at the bottom, circling there for a moment, knowing the falls had to be braved, knowing the fall wasn't fatal. But realizing it's good practice, knowing I'll be going over the last possible edge soon enough. Floating out in a widening delta where the flood slows, thinking, I want to hold on as long as I can.

'Wanting sometimes makes the difference,' says the young voice of the nurse. 'Haven't you drifted off to sleep yet?'

'Where did everyone go?'

'I told them they could see you tomorrow. You can hardly keep your eyes open.'

It's true. I'm yawning. 'It's the pills,' I say.

'It's the exercise. Sleep well,' she says, and slides away into the silence beyond my view. The curtain falls in folds that sway and sway before they too become silent. A shadow flickers on the wall as she passes through the door I cannot see.

The soft noises of night seem not to make any impression against the quiet that surrounds me. I have tumbled down that long river and into the ocean. Into the sea of dreams? Maybe. Into the sea of understanding? Perhaps no more than a momentary calm, but I ride its surface while I can.

I still don't have all the answers. Is that all I can add to the impervious questions, another negative? But maybe there is something to be said for silence. Maybe this peace of mind is the place I wanted to be.

Out on the waves are riding the tiny fragile boats in which my children sleep, my husband weeps, my parents sigh and wait. I am swimming toward them, slowly and with no sense of effort. As if the current from that river of tears that washed me from the cold highlands to the warm living sea has its shadow in the ocean, pushes me the way I want to go, co-operates with me in my slow struggle to understand.

My eyes are open to the pale folds of the curtain, the ceiling fanned with dim light; my ears are open to the sounds of the hospital night. But like the ocean water the whole world surrounds me. I can see far more than the pallid details of the darkened room. Overlapping memory and vision enrich the night. Without knowing how I did it, I've returned, chosen life while I have a choice. Maybe I was too tired to resist any more the flow of the world against my skin, all of my senses. And so, I seem to have a new contract. Maybe I signed the papers without knowing it.

Not that anything changes – much. But a little is a lot when the routine has become so pervasive. The routine of numb submission, the routine of going through the motions. After weeks like that, any change relieves the boredom.

Boredom? That I realize was part of it. But surely now I can stay interested long enough to end it well. If I have to end it at all, go out happy not laughing. Leave the ones who love me with something more than fat woman fiction.

The curtain's still folds, the light on the ceiling, the sounds from the corridor, all fade to darkness and deep silence. But I am not alone. Against the grainy tapestry of night there is a spread of bright detail. I want to see it better before I choose night altogether. I want to spend some time with it.

Time. Where I began, not ready then to accept that time is not voracious but only ubiquitous, like the layer of water that covers our world, or like the layer of flesh which used to insulate me from my life. Like that flesh my time has been eaten away, but it is not all gone. Tonight I have been away and above and into time. Looking down from those highlands where I was hiding, I would be able to see the eminence of my life as such a small island in that sea. Sinking into the water, until one day I will vanish altogether. But I cannot think of that now. I am drowning not in death but in sleep.

Greedy for morning, my eyes fall shut, and I let them, thinking, I may as well enjoy the time. I don't have much more of it.

Columbus Hits the Shoreline Rag

> ' . . . and the fiddler played a tune
> at a quarter past noon
> called "Columbus Hits the Shoreline Rag" . . . '
> A. Fraser

WHAT DO YOU SEE WHEN YOU TURN OUT THE LIGHT? (a bay in the New World)

I was down below the edge of the world and looking for a way back up when Isabella called me, she said
  alright, let's get some action here
  what's bugging you baby
  About time we cleared up this flat earth crap
so she put me on a ship and tripped me off to foreign climes and that's how I got where I am today.

Isabella thinks I found it on purpose, of course. She doesn't know how much time I was spending in the after stores consoling myself with the storeskeeper, a tubercular young man who fortuitously looked a great deal like the girl I had been forced to leave behind me – well, you know, it's the same old sad story, and that's where I was when the cry went up and the crash came.

I emerged on deck quite *déshabillé* to realize that the ship was no longer moving, that tedious cresting and troughing,

in point of fact we had run aground, and all sorts of quite
bizarre really and rather naked personnages were clustered
around the bow making savage-sounding chitchat which I
was totally unable to decipher. I sent the cabin boy (he'd
do anything for me) down to my quarters for the universal
translator and gradually it all came clear to me –
  wow
  far out
  What IS that?
  must be a UFO
  never saw an unidentified floating object quite that big
  Suppose those are real people?
  nah, it's all done with holographs
  yeah, when I was up in Disney World last winter, you
know the stuff up there you just wouldn't
  Hey, that one's saying something
  far out, they talk too! And the lips are in sync
  Don't be stupid, it must be real. Have you ever seen an
illusion with its fly undone.
  – so I pulled myself together and made some speech or
other and when I saw this quite luscious young thing on the
edge of the crowd dressed in really a rather informal way
and of course the crew was restless after all that time on the
roving main so to speak so I declared shore leave for the
whole fleet (the other ships by this time having anchored
in the bay).
  Well. You can't imagine the way the men cheered, and
the natives, after a moment
  (well, I never, just like that, without a by-your-leave
  I bet they don't even ask before they raid the fridge
either)
  were quite complimentary –
  Suppose we should Make Welcome
  guess so
  Chief?
  after you my dear councillor
  why not have some young person give an appropriate

of course my lovely daughter would be more than happy to

oh mother!

do what I tell you, girl

(oh all right) O wayfarers from the lands far away across the sea we the people of these united islands welcome you in the name of etcetera etcetera and invite you to share with us the fruits of our land

(at this the storeskeeper looked interested)

the game on our table

(what game? said the second mate

blackjack of course, only game in town, replied the councillor, sotto voce, as we say at home)

the hospitality of our yurts and so forth. Do please disembark from yon bark.

(of course all the men by this time had leaped overboard onto the sand)

and have ye a great old time, taking proper precautions whilst so doing as we have stabilized the birth rate and are trying very hard to maintain a balanced post-transitional ecology.

– and who could refuse an offer like that?

It was while they were putting together the bacon sandwiches and we were passing out the carbonated drinks that the mate, a chummy sort of fellow really, went to the chief and asked for her daughter's hand in marriage, the chief by this time quite soused on palm wine –

of course of course take all of her why don't you

!

stupid foreigners

– and as Captain of course I was approached to make with the dearly beloved we are gathered in order that they might then go off and consummate their union (I having been during this time absorbed in the exploration of new territory in the shape of a lovely morsel I'd seen in the welcoming crowd)

however

I recognized in the chief's daughter a certain resemblance to a girl I'd left pining in Barcelona and finding a spirit of co-operation lacking in the young thing I'd first found

(get your paws off me you old fleabag)

I sent it packing and ordered the mate back to the ship to stand watch

but Cap, he said

no buts I said accurate as usual as Sir Walter hadn't been invented yet

No no a thousand times she cried

but I was developing an acute sense of *droit de seigneur* and in the end

TOUGH TITTY SAID THE KITTY BUT THE MILK'S ALRIGHT (an island, ibid)

It was not long afterward that I was approached in my palm frond hut by the head of the Social Anthropology team to discuss a matter of cultural import.

Seems our closely (but apparently insufficiently) monitored shore leave was tending to disrupt the natural tribal patterns of the natives to such an extent that they were finding serious strictures beginning to affect the ordering of their reality such that the established ethical constructs that had sustained their culture thru the demographic transition and centuries of other difficulties were degenerating into an unprecedented shock reaction which if left to continue would tend to halt their hitherto unchecked forward evolution and place their society among the ranks of endangered social systems within a short period of time.

Moreover the chief herself appeared to make a statement about the prevailing social climate.

you have to get your disreputable crew out of here! And quit handling my daughter! Haven't you got any respect for our taboos? None of you gives a fig about

I really couldn't see what they all expected me to do about it considering that the seed had already been planted in more ways than one, and I myself in any case have always been in favour of the melting pot of society concept over the idea of maintaining cultural integrity, so with my free hand I waved them away

but, the chief said still lingering in the doorway, we've never done things this way

Tough titty, I said, continuing to caress her daughter lewdly, and motioning for the security team. Shove off.

And eventually we did.

WHAT DID YOU BRING ME FROM AMERICA DADDY? (Spain, some time later)

Chris, how lovely
isn't she
I mean, to see you. Who is she?
The lawful wedded widow of my first mate. I've been showing her around Barcelona.
she must be bringing in the ducats
oh, she does. Would you like her, Izzy?
Thank you so much! Where did you get her?
America
so you cleared up this nonsense about the edge of the world being just over the continental shelf
sure did. You proud of me?
oh, Chris, you know I am. What else did you find there?
Well. The natives have some simply charming customs, let me show you.
splendid! and when we get up we can hurry and discover tobacco and claim new lands and so forth
but in the meantime
(MUSIC. VIOLINS)

LIFE IS MUCH MORE FUN WHEN YOU'RE REFRESHED (San Salvador)

You're WHAT?

By who?
Those white-skinned barbarians?
don't give me that
well at least your sister didn't
What's that you're mixing with your palm wine?
Coca what Company?
(Dear Sirs. Please be advised that in accordance with accepted Foreign Policy and based on Information rec'd from various Explorers in the Region
(I have hereby claimed these Islands, heretofore to be known as San Salvador, and all those lands which Lie beyond, in the name of the King and Queen and the Sovereign Nation and So On, and do hereby establish thereupon this Colony,
(hoping you will see fit to send sundry Troops to hold the Settlement and for the Protection of the Natives)

I REMEMBER THE WINTER OF '92 (woodlands of – later – Alberta)

I was down below the edge of the world when the news came, I was lying under birch trees, let me tell you about the world
was sunshine and high summer
many fishes in streams
my mother soaking bark in the sun-warmed water curving it into baskets
my father and father's brother gone to the prairie after buffalo
o yes it was one idyllic scene, all right. Those days will never come again, little one
I was looking thru leaves at the sky and a hawk was circling, was thinking O what a beautiful morning o what a beautiful day! He was wearing next to nothing (our habit in those days) running down the path breathless
he said Hey!
whaa?

Hey, he said, hey! and I realized he was gasping and gave him some water and a neck rub and presently he said

America has been discovered

oh, I said, where?

Here, he said

whodunit? (my phrasing was classical)

hell, they say some Vikings popped in generations ago, but it's a bunch of Spaniards making the news now. I understand they're making a big fuss about the whole thing, and they're a real bunch of degenerates too, I'm told

He took off his loincloth to mop his sweaty brow and I said

well, that's it, then

I'm afraid so

how long have we got?

they won't get here in our lifetime, but we'd better teach the kids a thing or too. Mind you, there may be compensations. Already they've introduced some strange new customs into the civilized world, shall I show you?

I hardly know you

I'm your uncle's brother-in-law's cousin's son

from the sociologically differentiated tribe down the valley?

indeed

and these customs?

very interesting I think

So I turned off the universal translator and we communicated more subtly after that.

MY NAME IS OZYMANDIAS, KING OF KINGS
(Batoche, centuries later)

ouch

dammit, what now

I stubbed my toe, Daddy. On that nasty rock

That's not a rock, dear, it's an artifact

An artifact? You stubbed your toe on a goddamn artifact?
And how much is that going to cost me?

oh, hush, Ed, it's not broken

well, just pick up your feet

how come we're stopping here anyhow, Daddy?

There was some big Indian battle or something here.

Red Indians, Daddy?

don't bother your daddy now, dear. The bus ride made
him feel sick

mommy, I have to go to the bathroom

you'll have to wait for the bus to come back

but mommy, why?

there are no bathrooms here, this is a historic site

think we can see it all in twenty minutes, Sylvia?

it'll have to be a quickie

I hate these package tours

SET THE CONTROLS FOR THE HEART OF THE SUN
(the end)

I was down below the edge of the world when the call
came, looking for a way back, I flipped the switch and the
voice said

request permission to come

granted

aboard

sure (you see, I'd been having these dreams –)

and in they came, sifting thru the computer banks looking
none the worse for wear right from that first sad dark-
skinned beauty down to the intense Canadian kid with the
big voice and I said hi welcome siddown as they kept coming,
figuring it was near the end of the flight and when I was sick
of the illusion they'd all go away, maybe be replaced by
some of the tanned lovelies I saw in Florida when I was
training, o the nights at the Copacabana Motel, but no, an
orbit and a half later they were still there, so crowded I was
starting to worry about the oxygen, and not as transparent

as they'd been at first, for of course by then they'd gone
thru a good deal of past history, murmuring among themselves, and a good deal of my dehydrated food –

tastes like pemmican, said AV

been a long time, eh? said a woman

– and all the time looking at me just a little bit oddly –

I think we took them too seriously

you're not one to talk, Long Lance

well, you let them put you thru school, so

It's all a matter of whose reality triumphs (that was the
old man in the white shirt and pants)

but he looks so real (the first woman)

of course I am, it's you people who are the big dream.
Why don't you buzz off, anyhow? It's almost time for me
to start re-entry

– looking at me oddly, and then they started playing with
the switches, not fading away at all, and finally Mission
Control called up (I always like that phrase) called up
(everything is relative anyhow) called up and said what
the hell are you doing up there playing button button? your
brain wave monitors have gone crazy, your payload has
increased, however the hell you managed that, you've just
left orbit, and you've hit the manual override, so we can't
take over from you. Have you finally gone bonkers? Pull
yourself together! and one of them grabs the mike and it's –

Ermineskin here, friend. Just call me chief

– what? –

A few of us decided to come on up here and get into the
action

right on

shhh

and we're wondering what there is to discover up here

– whaa? –

After all, you discovered us, now it's our turn

Right!

shhh

– come off it, how are you doing all those different voices? –

We are (he continued, reading from a hide handed to him – thanks, Long Lance) we are the victims of overwhelming cultural genocide and we have at the last possible moment rallied and have decided to make the biggest gesture of our collective career and this particular co-operative inter-national endeavour is just the right vehicle. So if you'd kindly lay on the media coverage we can get on with it.

– That's all very well said Mission Control but at the moment your fancy fingerwork has screwed up the course so much that if you don't get that astronaut back in control the whole damn thing's gonna burn right up and then where will you be o noble savage and all that? Not to speak of hijacking and kidnapping and how the hell you got up there in the first place –

that was uncalled for, said AV and cut the communi-cations off, then thought better of it and grabbed the head-set, turned on the switch and began crooning wordlessly into the mike

hey, what are you – I said, and he looked at me oddly. Again.

Waddya think, pasteface, I'm chanting. Tradition has it that

They're just a big delusion! Just ignore them, Mission Control, come in Mission Control, they'll go away eventu-ally, you know these dreams I've been having, it's all just a

Shut up, man, you're screwing up my song

dream, there ain't any Indians up here, none at

could somebody get this nuisance out of here? (one with an American accent)

The way to deal with us is not by ignoring us (this was the one in the rusty black suit, Ermineskin had called him Long Lance). That just exacerbates the problem. I'm prepar-ing a long statement for the wire services. You may be interested in the analysis I make of the cultural precedents for, and the factors leading up to, our present actions. You know, there was a time when I really thought we could work with you people, but now I

c'mon, man, cool it

look, Voice, this celebration song business can go too far. We've hardly started. Besides I need the mike to read my news release.

shit, man, I was just getting into it! What kind of Indian are you anyways?

I'm with you all the way, you know that, we discussed all this

Haven't you all received enough recognition in the last few years to make up for it? I said trying to grab AV's arm my hand sliding thru

besides, you may find us capable of ignoring you, and you will become the history that never happened (the one with the Spanish accent)

– Mission Control calling, Mission Control calling, acknowledge, acknowledge –

can't you hear that?

man, I can only hear Cree

– acknowledge, important course correction in three minutes, C minus three minutes and counting, mark, are you there, acknowledge –

that so? I'm a Yaqui, myself

Iroquois

can't you hear (I feel myself getting hysterical) listen, if you don't let me make that correction we'll

don't sweat it, man, relax. You're coming apart anyhow. Gitchie Manitou'll take care of it

burn up, listen to me, what is it you people want anyhow? Can't you

AV, I think you've got a great idea, let's all sing a bit of a

listen to me! Don't you know we're not the same ones? You can't blame us for what some sixteenth-century barbarians did! We can't be responsible for the mistakes of our forefathers

don't forget foremothers, there

aaaaaaaaaahhhhhhhhhh, ahhahhohhhooohhh

don't you know that all the astronauts in the Canadian space program except me are Caughnawaga Mohawks, nobody else can stand the heights, what more do you

oh, shut up, man, we've had it with your buzzing

you're all going to die, what kind of dumb gesture is that, why don't you just hit that remote switch there, see, I'll let you do it all by yourselves, no interference, isn't that enough of a

what's that funny humming noise, man?

oh, nothing, Voice, just ignore it and it'll go away

Long Lance, you said you could work with us

(Not now, sorry, I've chosen the Indian way. I've gone too far now. Happy trails) What's that tune, Geronimo? Cochise? Ermine?

– Mission Control calling! Course correction minus ten seconds and counting, nine, eight –

What's that red light, Juan?

that's not important. Keep singing

hey, what's happening to me, what's

– five, four, three –

Say, this is far out, eh, Long Lance? Look at that view

It certainly is a giant step for the Indian Confederacy. Capital idea of yours, Voice

Thanks, man. Hey, look at that

– Mission Control calling, please acknowledge, you have missed course correction, please jettison pod, jettison immediately, you are in dangerous proximity to the sun's gravitational field, you are in dangerous –

hey, man, look how close we are!

wow

Far out!

Let's get that counterpoint going again, people, c'mon

ahhaayyahhaayyy

– proximity to the sun –

It seems to be warming up some, Spotted Calf

Sure is, Big Bear. Just breathe deep and keep chanting

I hereby claim this Fiery Ball in the name of the Indian Sovereign Nations and do give it the Name of Sun, Life-Giver, and do here establish the first Colony in the name of all Brothers and Sisters of our Nations and of the Gitchie Manitou, by whatever name each calls the Spirit

Hey, Ermie, it's getting hot in here, man, isn't there any more water?

Just relax, Voice, keep chanting, it'll be alright soon, everything'll be okay as soon as we

the white city

**(Report on the Expedition to Earth
to Examine the After-effects of
Armageddon on San Francisco)**

there's a central silence here where I sit with the
crystal ball in my hand. I don't want to mislead you, darling,
it's a small crystal, I can curl my hand almost over it. through
its depths all I can see is my palm made large and incompre-
hensible. if you were to read it now, it could say nothing to
you.

I have been down the road and back again, through the
forest of thoughts until I rest again in the centre, the ball in
my hand.

last night we were in a fast car on a long road in Italy.
where are we going? I said, but I kept driving, pushing the
car fast through the smooth fields. past us going the way we
came rolled, not cars, but three balls, strung out in a line,
first one, then two close together. I turned to you and said,
decide what you want, and do it.

you showed me plans of that house on the cliff where the
rich woman lived with her adult children. you didn't like the
way I behaved, arguing with them about the privilege of
wealth, flaunting the ultimate bad taste of my poor family,

arguing – it doesn't matter, we were soon gone from there, streaming down the long road, through the fields, toward the white city we could see from those heights. down past the long arm of ocean that imitated a river. the sun was golden behind the crags where so recently we had stood, beside the beautiful house of the rich woman and her two children.

the road was shining and very smooth. faster and faster I pushed the car. we stopped for water at a farm house. a beautiful young girl ran away at our approach. a suspicious woman was lulled into smiles by our politeness. we do not talk about the dead children. she would only suffer needlessly, for her daughter is still alive. we flow on toward the shining city, past the spheres rolling the way we came, the rising sun white and the fields gleaming and beyond the fields on the right, on the north-west, the sea in a long shining arm outflung over the land. Italy. a land shining, in my eyes.

we sail across the bright ocean, a boat silent and gentle and inexorable taking us to the heart of the golden-white sphere of the horizon, the sun. the woman in the bow, who has left behind her two children. the crystal in my hand, focussing the intense rays into a pain of light come burning into my palm, even though I close my hand on the ball of light, hold it away from me, look back at the windows of the house on the cliff where the rich children are still arguing about privilege.

out here the wind is so strong that it makes a central silence. it's not a true dream, it's an idea I read somewhere. I am sailing away from you. you were the sinking island where mariners could never land. you left me in my small boat in the centre of the sea. the gold sun shining on the far Italian city, so far away now. left behind on another world. in my palm nothing but a sphere of glass, finger-printed and flawed slightly, to make a darkling shadow in the middle, a point of privilege.

clouds in the goldness. shadows on the serene ocean. we

have come to a sere land, the woman has stopped crying over her family, she steps down quietly onto the sand. the sun relentless in my palm. one can catch diseases in foreign lands, from objects one finds there. I have caught the disease of dreaming, from you, my beauty, my almond-eyed one; you never answer a question with anything but a question / you reprove me for my fast driving. I swear I will do better, but I love the fans of sand thrown up by the tires, I love the road I am leaving behind me, from the beach where the ship is lying over, beached, yes, stranded, that white strand. the sun.

horizon line in the small crystal which so round I can hold it in the very centre of my hand, curl my long fingers over the image in its centre, ignore the pain. driving up over a bluff and into the forest, the map you folded for me now swelling into a living thing, growing into a tree, a flower, a living road, the trees a tracery of bare branches, uncomplicated by life.

we are moving as fast as we can across the dangerous surface of the world. a group of people eating lunch, *le déjeuner sur l'herbe*, are startled by our approach until we ask them for directions, and they show me in the ball the correct road, which descends through my palm and into the earth. their faces grave and questioning. do you know? I tell them that I too came from a simple family, we went often to the park to play. often to the wood to live. their children have wandered off into the trees, we go and look for them. the picnickers are frightened, the clouds blow, the rain falls.

in the car we close the windows, the dusky smell of the woman overwhelms me. the searchers are left far behind, finding their children in the water, face down, floating, their striped rubber balls bobbing beside them. the Italian farmer's child streaks like a golden line through my memory. the woman with me wants to know if the car is all right. the long bonnet cuts through the rain. her smell is powerful and strong. I can feel how much I want her, but there is no place to stop. I am driving in a narrow trail, leaning over the wheel to see through the rain, wanting the sunny fields and the house where she lived on the cliff, where I argued with her children, where we could have laid down in perfume and shameless sex. her black hair is drawn back from her face. she takes the sunglasses from her bag, puts them on. her infrared vision sees danger. I hold the crystal up past the mirror. the ray of light spears through the storm. I do not like the way this darkness is going. growing. the light as strange as laser rays, the mirage in the sky appearing: the white city, reversed, meaning the abode of death, the end of delight. the card that crosses it is the sun, the only influence we have. the crystal against my pale hand, the light bounding from my pain and out into the clouds.

not far now. the devastation of the city is complete. the falling stones and rubble bury the children's bus, the cries of the parents, the bustle of the stock exchange: gone, and the flood washes suburbia into the grey ocean.

not far from the coast now, the woman says. I know you are waiting in the depths of the spherical light, waiting on the coast with your warm smile. you are crazy to live like this, you said, while I packed the medical supplies. we came down in Italy, where the news had not yet arrived. I drove across this wide sphere for the truth, for you, for all the riches I lacked as a poor child. the woman had a husband. he gave me a handsome gift when we arrived, and spoke in a language I had not rehearsed. even though I was mute with him, the woman believed me, and she came aboard the ship though the sun still shone on her home on the cliff.

no use looking back. only sadness to remember the vivid anger with which I argued, her arrogant children gleaming in the sun. but now she is with me in the darkness, the road breaking into smaller and smaller pieces, the glass ball in my hand, my hand so tired and burning, so cold and stiff.

how foolishly I pursue her in my thoughts, no place to stop, to take her silk shirt from her shoulders and let free her round breasts, to peel the smooth skirt from around her brown thighs, those long legs surround me, those long lashes open and close for me, I know every molecule of her transparent body, there is nothing we can do for the walking dead.

the car is tearing away from around us. you showed me the plans, told me it would never last through the winds. I hold the lamp of my small sun ahead of us, above us, and we walk further and further toward the coast. again and again the light pierces the mirage of the white city. the rocks are warm and hurt my feet. the woman's arm is cold. the storm is clearing around us as we mount the rise from which we will first see the water.

across the sinister ocean the fog recedes. the wind at our backs now. the broken city lies around us, shrouded in the souls of the children. it is always the future which suffers. the devastation of the rift between the past and the present. too much philosophy for you, my darling, you told me I should never make this journey. we could have happily stayed in that beautiful house on the jagged cliff, watching the sun set rays to warm the white city.

but I came from a poor family. I cannot rest safely on the mountain.

there is a place in the ruins where the woman and I can lie down. her mouth comes down on me in anger – it is not at all what I wanted, it is nothing like I feared. then the sun has exploded again, and we go streaming down toward the coast, flowing in the channels of the melted city, flowing in the path of destruction, sparkling with the radiant light of the small cloned sun.

you are waiting smiling by the shore. the woman walks before me, crying for the dead. she steps into the boat, where it rocks on the still water. the fire has melted the sand of the beach into a glassine road. leading to hell, I say. I've made hell portable, you say, let me show you the plans. you unfold the road before me, and it is the track of the rising dying sun across the unaroused ocean. I look into the crystal and see the white city, drowning, sinking into the phlegmatic water, the burnished light of the sun making fires of its glistening rooftops above the mirror of the sea.

behind us the ruins of the dream city split with a grand explosion along the fault line, sink with a stately sigh into the tide. we are sailing into the rising ocean, the sun, the horizon a line curling into a curve in the sphere in my hand. the sphere reflecting only my magnified flesh, my hovering face, the dream at the end of life, when the cliff is brought down by the water as I knew it must be, the rich woman's children devastated, the handsome house lost and the ship adrift in flat antipodes where the rising sun burns/burned down the path of light and into my hand.

I came from a poor family, to this. you have turned the boat in the water, until the bow locks into that smooth road. plankton is growing like crops in the sea, we pass a farmer and her daughter, their smooth shining fins curl above the surface for a moment. we are sailing deeper and deeper, the sea rising, we are sailing into the white city at dawn, with the burnish of light making your eyes golden. the woman in the bow, her hair flowing in the wind of her passage. the sphere in my hand, silent and opaque, like your eyes, like the sea rising to meet us, taking care of us from now on. the white stones falling around us. the silence in the centre of the sphere in my hand, where I have read the dream, driving fast through the dream around the whole devastated world, finding no human child alive but the one golden child who waits for me now at the space in the centre of the city, reaching out to take from me the crystal, but I close my hand

and turn out the light on the last whited city, the final light of the last sinking dream.

THE FACE CARDS

the white city: life; reversed, death (or: death; reversed, life) the crystal sphere: the sun, the bomb, the life force, the soul, information; reversed, focus of devastation, epicentre of the blast, force of entropy

the ocean: death; reversed, rebirth

the dolphins: resurrection; reversed, alien dreams

the ship: escape and intensity; reversed, sensual destruction

the fast car: force of time, progressive differentiation; reversed, vulnerability

the driver: sex, honour and mortality; reversed, doubt and rumours of war

the woman: sex, mortality and belief; reversed, denial and doubt

the companion with the map: information theory; reversed, devastation

the road: inevitability, life, death, rebirth; reversed, inevitability, entropy, the funnel into the void

dreams: fate, distance, distinction, homecoming; reversed, visions, delusions, false journeys

By Their Taste Shall Ye Know Them

Boil 'til the flesh comes off the bones, he said, but it's not as simple as you might think, and frankly, even in a permissive society its bloody hard to get a permit for something so strange, no matter how good the cause. It's a lot of boiling, and the odour spreads, and the neighbours start looking a little off-centre – but that's how I spent the long weekend.

I considered putting a few carrots and onions in too, as a sort of gesture of respect, but when it came down to cutting them up, I found a carrot with two tails, looking fleshy and mandrakey, and I started feeling a bit queasy myself. Not doubting what I'd done really, but you know, you start thinking. Now they're saying plants scream when they die too, and advocating we recycle ourselves, our husks, so to speak, once we're through with them, toss ourselves back into the protein mill. What I want to know is, what do they say about the protein ratio then, 8:1 is it, or 10:1? So will we have to eat up our grandparents and several other old folks, just to reach our protein quota? Will there be eight times fewer of us every generation? And when the last nine are left, who'll be the lucky survivor still around to greet the rescuers from Earth – if they're real, and show up on the dot of the millennium, like they're supposed to?

I think the whole thing can go too far. Maybe its time that plants quit screaming and resigned themselves to their place in the natural order – like I'm gonna have to do, when my time comes. It'd kinda make my going easier to think that I might be served up with a lettuce side salad, or a few steamed carrots, and that my descendants won't be looking with hungry eyes at the next old bugger getting ready to go.

Well, no use thinking about that – I'm too young to worry, and the Bill isn't even through parliament yet. There I was trying to cook up the – well, meat, not to put it too bluntly – and spending the whole weekend on it, because when you get a great hunk of flesh like that, a couple of hours isn't gonna reduce it to stock.

That Samuel was a hefty old bugger, I have to say it, though he was a good friend to me, helped me out of a lot of hot spots, so to speak. And really, it was his last wish, and I was doing my best to render him as was his due.

Now, I'm not sure I believe in Earth, but Sammy did, and claimed he could remember his old grandsire telling him all about it. And Sammy was not a fabricator. I knew that for a fact, having seen him once get battered to within an inch of life because he wouldn't lie about some little matter – whether he felt potatoes screech when he ate them, probably. This world's in a hell of a mess, and it goes like that sometimes.

It's been a few hundred years since the world was settled. Things change, stories change, and the real facts get forgotten. The way Sam told it we are descended from the ones they had to leave behind, and a sad story too, with the children weeping and the adults saying 'I promise, no matter how long it takes, even if it takes a thousand years . . . ' Of course, Sammy's story is more like the new kids' version, the Revised Standard text, and it's considerably simpler than the rhyming quatrains I had to learn in training, hundreds of them in the whole story. In the sanctified version, we were already here when they came, and we intermarried and were changed. No hint of inequality in those – the Faith has decided it wouldn't contribute to the proper attitude at the millennium.

Maybe I'll still be alive then if I eat enough carrots or potatoes or grandparents by then. I tasted a bit of Sammy's stew, but it was greasy and heavy and the meat was stringy. Not like vegetables at all.

He knew what he would cook up like, though. It was in one of his old books, the one he read and reread. It contained rituals from the old time; it was printed and bound before all the presses were needed for the more important ecclesiastical books and papers. It was in these rituals that most mention was made of the role we used to play in the lives of the ones who departed.

On the weekends Sammy and I would study together, though we had to keep quiet about it, on account of my job, which is in the Sacred Library, and I'm not supposed to know that those books exist outside of the Rare Book Room, which is locked.

So why did I do it? Well it gets back to the books, really, and the way I felt about him, lardy old bugger he turned out to be.

Sammy taught me that when there was time for celebration, like Crystalmass when the geodes came together, one of the company who had recently died would be prepared, with offerings of food, to be served up to the company, as a communion of Strength and good wishes. At first the idea made me a bit ill, with the laws and Sacred Rules the way they are, but Sammy helped me see the sense in it, all that protein being wasted when it could have helped them go on another day without using the hydroponic garden, and it would have been freely given too. About then I'd read about how the plant savers started claiming it was murder to eat vegetables, started this octogenarian business (or at least, Sammy used to call it that, referring to their proposed alternate diet) and somehow after a while it didn't seem as strange.

'The thing is,' said Sammy with concern on his wide old face, 'we've changed. Hundreds of years on this planet, the hard radiation, even you know that our parents were smaller, and theirs smaller than them, and we seem to be getting hairier, or maybe smoother, one or the other; no one has done anything empirical to prove it either way. Hard too, the way organic matter decomposes. But the old paintings seem to show us as very different.'

'The thing is,' he said, passing his wide horny hand over his eyes and snout, 'how will they know they've come back? They're real, here's the proof, in these pictures, but how will they know this is the same place they left hundreds of years ago? We've changed so. We'll have to be able to tell them.'

So the long and short of it is, he made me promise. I prepared the mixture like he said, 'seasoned water' he called it, and put him in, and boiled it as the old books say. And if my time is nearly up before they've come, I'll choose some promising young one and pass along the trust.

'You must promise me you'll keep it for them, to offer them when they come.' He was feverish at the end and rolled his big old body around and around on the bed. 'You must have it there, to offer them when they come, so they'll know it's us, and take us home with them as they should have done.'

'I promise,' I said, first to quiet him, but then I realized I meant it. Really meant it. For his sake.

'I'll do it,' I promised. 'Even if I lose my job and they all think I'm nuts.'

'They won't,' he said. 'They'll just think you've joined the anti-plant-murder movement. They won't know the real reason.' And he smiled, and he died right there, with a joke.

Which is why, when he died, I cut him up, like he asked, got the permit and boiled him in the big pot 'til the meat came off the bones. I froze the stew and kept the bones, and now I wait. Wondering if he's wrong or right, and whose grandparent I'll live to be.

So when they come floating down at the millennium with their hair all misty around their smooth cold faces will they know us, and want to take us away like they promised? And is it really home, like Sammy said, and would I want to go?

Willows

On my home planet there are still poplar forests, with willow bushes growing beneath near the banks of small streams. When I am home I stay in a holiday home made of logs. It is a gigantic place, with many guest rooms, most of them empty now, and a large local staff. An antique, as I am, a lucky leftover from a distant past, it stands on a bluff above a deep-cut creek bed, in the midst of a grove of these white smooth poplar trees. When I have reconciled with gravity and become strong again, I walk down the zigzag paths from the top of the bluff until I am standing by the ice-bound water. I am usually there in winter or early spring, and under the ice I hear the creek's trapped singing. On the snow are animal tracks. Twigs fallen onto the drifts have retreated deep into tiny sinkholes just their shape. I bend over to study how a twig lies in a forked trough as deep as my fingers are long. I try to keep these memories current, have them nearby to replay when I am travelling out where snow would be impossibly warm and rabbits are unknown except as myth.

When I am replaying the memories I come to a moment when I must retell the story of the first guest who came with me to the lodge, and what came of it. That time, my eyes were new, and I had been gone longer than usual, but there was one other difference. I never speak of my career when I am there, for the people have been conservative in that country and I am never sure they approve of the ship or its mission. But this time I took with me, quietly, another spacer, a being from another colony, but enough like a man to excite no comment.

Yet if I speak of him as a man, which it would be so easy to do, I will lose the essential reason which, in the end, made the story more than a simple holiday. Nevertheless, I shall try, and see what comes of it.

He was tall for his people, tall for ours too, so that he bent his head to get through the doorways. But he was thin, and seemed on account of his shy manner not much of a threat. He at first knew little spoken language, so passed as a man from the other side of the world. He had never seen a tree before, but that is true of many in the Siberian archologies, so the people shook their heads and smiled and felt they knew who he was. At night in the room we shared he would talk for hours with his hands, for that was the language we had in common, but we didn't make much of our talking in company.

He understood skis very well, being accustomed to them at home, but even had I been ready for exercise, I have never been able to get the rhythm right, so different from the motions I have used all my life for getting around, so he took the skis every day and went by himself into the woods. At lunch and dinner he used to sketch out, with his limited words and with excited gestures only I knew were exclamations and descriptions, the vegetation and wildlife he had seen. The local people would tell him the names of what he had seen, its habits in the case of animals, and he would smile and dip his head and remember. The next day he would say: 'I saw a rabbit!', 'I saw a porcupine!', 'I saw a deer!' and then describe what it did.

The people patronized him, and so, I think now, did I, so much I took for granted the surroundings. No matter that I had been awed by the forms of life on many different worlds that I had in the end longed for poplar and willow and evergreen, rabbit and bird and deer, still I could not conceive that all these could be so strange to him or to anyone. But I had been asked to bring him with me, and to show him what I saw, so I was patient; and in fact, I grew to enjoy him, his ingenuous likings, his excited response. I imagine we like best the people who seem to love our homes, to see in them what we see. And he had a natural kindness which came through in small acts of civilized behaviour, so he seemed at home himself.

There was, staying at the lodge, another stranger: a woman of late middle-age, her grey hair long and braided and slightly untidy, for she too spent much of her day in the forest, off the paths. She often came home with her hair snagged by twigs and snow caked on her mountaineer's stockings and dry dead leaves clinging to her woollen sweaters. She seemed the complete outdoors-lover, there to hike and breathe, but she showed an extreme interest in the conversations my friend had with the local people, and she never talked about her own work, only questioned my friend on what he had seen that day, or made obscure jokes and laughed at them alone heartily while we all sipped our tea and smiled into our cups.

When first I return to the Earth I have to get used to not only gravity but company. Out in the ship, when I am travelling, it seems that I am the centre of everything, and it is not easy to remember that there are planets full of people all around the universe, none of them living or dying by my breath. Then when I come back it seems I am reluctant to give up my solitude, afraid of truly being sucked down into gravity. It makes it no easier to have to reclaim so many memories before I can fully arrive. So at first I watch, and go through the motions expected of me, and collect what I can in memory. On this visit, I was even more reluctant to become known, for I had been away longer than usual. I performed my re-entry rituals quietly, and alone.

After lunch it was my habit to take a thick woollen fringed robe and go out onto the veranda where I would tuck myself into a lounge chair like an old-fashioned tuberculosis victim taking the cure. Sometimes I would watch the chickadees in the nearby trees, augmenting my vision when I had to in order to look closely at their feathers and feet. Sometimes I would watch my friend ski through the trees, see him stop to look at something, then I would sharpen my gaze enough to see what he saw, would share with him the wonder of the moment. I was not walking strongly myself yet, but I with my new eyes could see a great deal without exertion. I never saw the stranger in her walks; perhaps she went, not down into the valley that I overlooked, but back onto the flat land behind us. Sometimes I fell asleep on that balcony, a deep, dream-filled sleep which left me refreshed and ready for the pre-dinner gymnasium workout which was acclimatizing me to my regained weight. It was a peaceful time.

My friend seemed to be getting what he wanted. I was still no more in tune with his ultimate goal, but I have learned over my career not to ask questions and not to speculate unless I have sufficient reasons or evidence, and I had neither. I was, after all, on vacation.

If events were building to some climactic moment, therefore, I did not see them, or, seeing them, would only recognize afterward that yes, this fits as a motive, or no, that wasn't part of the story.

One day very early in our stay, in February, he came back with a willow twig in his hand. It was about four inches long, forked and with a trace of lichen hanging green and lacy on the fork, and on the branches buds were bursting into softness. I have never ceased with a small part of myself to be amazed, for I remember when pussy willows – for that was what he had found, the spring's first pussy willows – were

April events. But much has changed since I was young, and much time has gone, and many willows budded since then.

'What is this?' he asked at the dinner table.

'Pussy willow,' said one of our hosts, smiling a tongue-in-cheek smile. 'That's where kittens grow.'

My friend looked from her face to the two lodge kittens who were rolling about chasing a fluffy something. They were grey and pudgy and not unlike the buds on the small branch. He then looked at me and I made a negation with my hands, smiling also. 'It's what we tell our children,' I said. 'I heard it too, when I was young.'

'But these are not animals?'

Before I could answer him the stranger came into the room, combing her hair with her fingers, an abstracted look on her wide face. When she saw the branch in my friend's hand, she seemed for a moment like a cat herself, a larger more threatening one. She pounced upon him, snatching the twig from his hand.

'Where did you get this?' she demanded.

Taken aback, he was unable to speak aloud. Across the creek, his hands said.

'Very well, don't tell me,' she said. 'I will find it. I have time. There must be a profusion of them, for you to be able to break a branch so carelessly.' And throwing down the twig in frustration, she stormed out of the room, back to the porch where she had just left her heavy boots, and we heard her putting them on.

Another of the local people went to the door. 'What about your lunch?' he asked.

'I don't need it,' she said. 'Feed it to the humans.'

And she slammed the door behind her.

My friend signed to me the surmise in both our thoughts, but I shook my head and shrugged. I thought this planet was not usually visited, he said then, and again I gestured my bafflement. 'Never mind,' I said, 'no doubt we'll hear about it later.'

'Is it wrong to break the branches?' he asked.

'Not unless it was the last branch,' I said.

'Is it the last branch?'

'I doubt it. The forests are healthy again now. Don't worry.'

Somone was playing the piano as we ate. It is a skill that has died out among the Terrans who travel. We listen to electronically-generated tones that sound like piano, but we have lost the reality. That is why I come here, to get back my reality. My friend was fascinated with the machine, and he soon was asking the musician to explain it to him. His hands are similar enough to human hands, only appearing double-jointed and unusually flexible, and they are long-fingered, ideal for a pianist. Soon he was learning finger exercises and in a few days, by the time I was strong enough to take short walks on the flatland, he was spending half the morning inside practising.

We had discussed the stranger, but neither of us could observe any evidence that she was not just an eccentric human. And if she was alien, as her remark had suggested, what of it? My friend too was alien, here for his own reasons, which were likely much the same as mine: to rest and be refreshed. If another visitor had found something to seek on my planet, who was I to worry?

Yet I did worry a little. I found myself curious and some-what on guard, and I made a point of watching her more closely now that I was outdoors more. When I went upon the flatland, I never saw her, and since I was not strong enough yet to go down into the valley, I could not test my assumption that she must be there, looking for the willow bushes perhaps, though it seemed inconceivable that she could not find them, for every willow now was budding. She never came to lunch, and at dinner she had a concentrated and distant look, her face wrinkled into a half-scowl, ignoring us all and speaking little or not at all.

Meanwhile my friend was also finding what he wanted. Mornings he practised his piano-playing (the willow twig with its furry blossoms in a glass of water beside him) and

I was amazed at his progress. So was his impromptu teacher, who called him 'a natural' and boasted about him to the others until complete strangers coming into the lodge would say to him, 'So, how's the music coming?' He reacted like a shy adolescent, smiling and seeming to blush. I used to tease him about it at night. Never mind, he would sign, having learned the phrase from me, they like to see me that way. And I enjoy it.

What, the playing? Or the play-acting? I asked. One of the kittens was in the room, trying to climb the bedspread. He picked it up and put it in his lap, where it batted at his signing hands.

Both, but the music more. I like your planet. I like your people.

I wish they were mine, I said. It is so long ago that I left. Only the trees and the wildlife are the same now.

You should make some new friends, he said.

He put a hand on my shoulder, a rare gesture (he was learning gestures too, here). I smiled and shook my head. When I looked at him he was studying me like a twig or a leaf. Or a rabbit, to see what I would do next. The warmth swept away from my back, and I shivered and threw my head back as if cornered. He dropped his hands into the placid, static sign for Don't worry. I shook my head again, this time brusquely, but his hands only pushed the same sign toward me. Finally I nodded and turned away to prepare for bed.

'I'm sorry,' I said without looking at him. 'I forget.'

'You may think me dangerous,' he said, 'But I am not without conscience.'

'How much your language has improved,' I said impulsively.

'Yes,' he said, and he put the cat into the corridor, closed the door and turned out the light.

In the next few days there was a cold wind from the southeast, and after the first morning I learned again to bundle up for my walks. I had enough strength now to try walking into the valley, though I knew the first day that I would be exhausted before I got home. As I stood on the lip of the bluff, looking at the zigzag path, one of the local people from the lodge came to stand beside me.

'Are you walking down today?'

'I think so,' I said.

'Good,' she said. 'You're coming along quickly. Would you like some company?'

'Well . . . '

'Just in case. Gravity will be your enemy on the way back.'

She was wearing an old, old-fashioned canvas coat, and her hands were burrowed into the pockets. She had a striped hat and blue jeans. She looked like someone from my past. She saw me looking at the hat.

'I made it myself,' she said. 'From the patterns you left last time.'

'You weren't here then,' I said.

'I was still a baby,' she said. 'But my father was your trainer then. This was his coat. I wear it when I miss him.'

'I thought I was being subtle,' I said. 'I'm doing it all myself, didn't even bring a trainer this time.'

'Only another one like yourself. Where was he from, Russia? Or China? No, too tall. Not this continent, though, because of the language.'

'They were tall, in the north of China. The Mongols.' If she wanted to think he was another like me, that was best. I began to pick my way down the ski trail into the valley. She followed me, quiet for the most part, but now and again pointing to something she thought particularly interesting. I too stopped often to look closely at some detail, storing the impression, focussing on every texture and shape. The wind was cold from down the valley, and my eyes smarted from its demanding force. At least, I felt it must be the wind causing the tears in my eyes.

A few days later a wind from the west brought warmer air. The densely growing poplars near the lodge were young and straight. Their trunks and leafless branches swayed restively in the wind. At their feet, the snow was slowly melting away until the tunnels mice make in snow-drifts were unroofed, and fallen leaves and dry grasses were revealed.

Day after day fell into the same comfortable pattern. In the morning, while my friend had his piano lesson and practice time, I walked alone on the flat land to the north of the lodge. Sometimes I walked all the way to the edge of the prairie, several hundred metres away. I say prairie, but really it was the edge of cultivation, where the fences and fields began, where the discipline of civilization had been imposed. There between the trees and the tilled earth, I was seen by no one.

By midmorning my friend was out of the house, and we would meet and walk, taking a different path each day. He asked many questions, but he soon learned that I could not answer the more probing ones: why did the branches grow this way? what makes the willow flower like an animal? what is a bird call? who made those tracks? I love my land, but I know it as a tourist. If a chickadee comes down to a tree by me and makes its unmistakable call, I know by the sound and by its black head that I have seen a chickadee. But when I record the sights and sounds and smells of home to remember later on the ship, I am not critical or even curious. I do not need to know which flying shadow is a redpoll, what sound is what bird or animal, what type of sparrow came to the log near me to sing. It is all a picture for me, an environment, and the pieces could be magic and I still would not care. Home, they used to say, is where the heart is; it is not where the mind is, I would have added.

But he wanted to know everything.

One of the lodge people was old and knowledgeable, so after lunch my friend would go with him out on the veranda or into the nearby woods and there would learn all those things he could not learn from me. Meanwhile, I would poise myself on the brink of the hill. Every day the young woman would join me and we would walk down into the valley together.

Her name was Anna. Her family had lived in this area for generations. Though the children went away to study and work, at least one in each generation came back, to walk, hands in pockets, through the enduring woods. She was recently back from a long stay in the modern world, and her knowledge of this land was like mine: the treasured, half-remembered imprint of a long-ago childhood, revived by the sights and smells in the wood, by the sound and feel of boots crunching through the snow. We had much in common.

She was the only one in the lodge to mention my career, though there must have been more who knew, as they were family to those who had been my hosts before. But she seldom asked me about my life, for which I was grateful; instead we talked about the surroundings and left the past to itself. She was reticent about her own past too, hence I also knew little of her.

She was curious about the other visitor. 'Who is that strange woman in the climber's outfit?'

'I don't know. I myself wondered.'

'She has an unusual accent. I don't recognize it.'

'Nor do I.'

She looked at me and smiled. 'Do you know that you have an accent too?'

'Do I?' I didn't want her to go on.

'Luckily we keep the old language alive here.'

'Old language?'

'The kids in the city – you wouldn't understand a word they say. Fast, easy and smooth is their motto.'

Then she spoke a few words in a dialect so elided I could not recognize a single word. I leaned against the tree nearest me, a birch whose bark was riddled by the beaks of sapsuckers. My recording, however, was done through a blur of tears.

'What did you say?' I said, my face turned away toward the wood.

'I said,' and she faltered, 'I said you were fine for . . . eh, fun but you didn't . . . mm, didn't give a wedge a place to bite.'

'Meaning, you can't understand me?'

'Yes, in part.'

A little further, the path dipped toward the stream-bed, and there the beavers had been working, so that several trees lay felled and stripped of their branches. On the trunk of one of these fallen trees I sat down. Across the creek, the lodge loomed high above us on the bluff, and I could see a figure that might have been my friend leaning over the balcony rail. I sharpened my gaze and saw that it was him; he was watching us. I made him a sign of welcome, then I turned to Anna who still stood on the path.

'This is my home,' I said. 'Do you know what that means?'

'Yes,' she said. 'It means you have come back here now and again over a very long time. You hold to your pattern like these birds hold to their migrations, compelled to return even though when you return all has changed. The people you first knew are dead. But you can make new friends, like me.'

'That's a side issue,' I said. 'When I am travelling, I am filled with the latest technology and I am never out of date. Here, in those cities, where I dare not go because I cannot speak the language, the life of the world goes on without me. Only here in the backwoods can I pretend I am at home. I used to live in the city as a child. I came to these woods on my holidays, like now. They were never a permanent home. So I feel lonely. And old, too old for comfort.'

She walked to me and took my hand. 'I am sorry.'

'I didn't have to think about it until I began to care for you,' I said, bitterly conscious of my archaic speech. But I felt her warmth and her kind intentions. When I heard her words in modern dialect the final power of gravity gripped me; I felt I was drowning in the sea of air, sinking slowly to the very bottom of the gravity well. Finally, always, I cannot deny my beginnings, or my yearnings. 'Come, let's go back,' she said, and I stood up.

Only then I noticed a noisy progress toward us through the bush: the stranger came with her hands full, it seemed, of lace.

'Look,' she said, and into our hands which we held out reflexively, side by side, she poured a collection of green lichen. 'Look, it's alive!'

Obediently we looked into our hands, but she shook our forearms with a strong hand each, and said, 'No, you fools, look around.'

'Of course it's alive,' I said. 'It always has been.'

'Don't be stupid,' she said. 'That was pure luck. Don't you know if there's destruction of the ecology, these are the first to go? I remember a time when nothing could be touched because it was so rare. But now, there are so many that I can collect them. I have never seen that before, any of the times I have studied this place. And you don't even notice. Can you say what has changed since the last time you were here?'

'I'm not likely to remember the last time. I've used it up,' I said.

'Oh, yes,' she said, 'the proverbial slippages of reality. But you could at least pay attention now.'

'I am remembering what I can,' I protested, not sure why I felt pressed to argue.

'Of course, but are you thinking about it, or just storing up your romantic fantasies? Never mind, never mind. You don't remember, so you keep your illusions that the forest was always so beautiful. I remember differently. Just think about how the forests have lived and thrived, and how little you used to expect of them generations ago. Now they are full of lichen to be played with. By me, who has never played with life before. Of course you don't know what it means, you' – she spoke to Anna – 'are only a young ethnolinguologist, and' – to me – 'you of course are just a sunburner here for a holiday. But you can rejoice anyway. The world will live through. It may even be here next time you arrive.' And she took back her samples of Old Man's

Beard (as my mother once taught me to call it) and was stuffing them into her pockets as she charged up the path toward the lodge.

'My secret it seems is no secret,' I said.

'Of course not,' Anna said. 'Every generation waits for your visit. You are our beloved spacer.' And she smiled, and we walked back home on the bustling trail of the stranger.

For many days I had left my companion much to his own devices. We spent time together, of course, for one does not forget one's friends, but I enjoyed the time for its immediate content, and ceased to wonder overmuch why he was here, why piano music, why pussy willows.

For there was no denying that he was fascinated by pussy willows. It was fully spring now, the snow mainly gone except under the south banks of the creek and the bluffs, and the forest floor and creek banks were mud and the beginnings of new growth. Above the valley across from the lodge, on the flat land at the other side, sloughs were melting and muskeg was waking up. There one day in my walk with Anna I saw a duck and a drake settle onto the calm face of the slough, and it was as if the ripples shook my life with the passing of time. Later, on the other shore of that grassy pond, I found a stand of willows whose blossoms were pink – why pink I do not know. They were some distance from the path through marshy terrain so I did not go close to them, but I remembered the place and took my friend there the next day. When we got there the sun was low and the pinkish-grey fur of the little flowers was gleaming. He was entranced, and almost waded across to the hummock where they grew, but I held him back. Coming home through the valley he detoured to the creek bank and ducked into a stand of willow there to stroke the furry blooms' softness, his thoughts obviously far from me. I took out my pocket knife, another antique, and going in beside him I cut a few branches. 'Come, we'll put them in water at home,' I said.

'That stranger seemed to say it was wrong to kill them,' he said.

'These will leaf in water, as the others did,' I said, for that first twig he had found had already begun to shed its fur for foliage. 'There are plenty here; you may as well have some at home with you if you like them so.'

Later, at home, he played more with one of the growing kittens and I wondered if for him there was still a connection. But when I asked him he only took the kitten into his lap, shook his head, and smiled.

We saw more and more of Anna, for she took to sitting down with the group after dinner. Once, my friend, responding to the requests of his older local friend, went to the piano to play, and, after listening for a few minutes, Anna began to sing. Her voice was a powerful contralto and the song, a slow ballad of loss and homesickness, brought tears to more eyes than mine. When she finished, we all applauded. My friend said something to her, but she shook her head, sat down and was silent, only smiling a little at one of the cooks who seemed to be her good friend. No matter how we asked her that and other nights, she would not sing again.

Anna talked to my friend almost as much as to me by now, and one evening she said, 'Stay up late tonight. The sky's so clear, and the moon will be full. It'll make a splendid midnight.'

'I am sorry,' he said to her quietly. 'I cannot look at the stars.'

'How about you?' she asked me.

'I think not,' I said.

She went away shaking her head, and the next morning she made a point of telling us what we missed. But in this my friend and I were alike and united: that we looked closer and closer to the ground the longer we lived upon it. The fine detail I was recording was building up in my thoughts. I would not shatter it with stars; not yet.

I had resisted as much as I could, but I was now beginning to learn the names of the local people, and their characters, and they, I imagine, found out something of me, for I spent much more time among them and almost stopped my solitary rambles. My friend too was more sociable, but there was still a distance, not as if they never made him welcome but as if he could not be welcome among them, never completely comfortable. Anna treated him gently, but he was very silent with her, conversations of smiles and gestures, as if they were building up their own sign language.

One day he said to me as we walked, now I see why you fit so well into your work.

It was the first time in weeks that he had talked of anything but the immediate experience, and I admit that I was shaken, for I had been trying to forget my career as much as I could now that my body had forgotten free fall.

What do you mean? I asked.

You have a gift for arriving in the environment, he replied, one I do not have. I cannot forget my home. I cannot forget what is different. But you have taken this into yourself.

But this is my home, I said, so it was in me already. But as I said it I was uncomfortable, for I knew there was much I wasn't remembering; I knew too that he could see my discomfort.

You have come as long a way as I to get here, he said. But you forget the distance and I do not. You continue to imagine yourself the centre of it. Have you ever seen my home planet?

I shook my head, and looked at him to continue, but he did not, and said no more on the subject for many days.

Time passed somnolently, as if slowly. All of us were relaxed. The stranger had become a known quantity, proven to be a naturalist, here to assess the degree of survival of the world's biosphere. There seemed no mystery there now. My friend was just a tall, piano-playing nature-lover who played with kittens and spoke with an accent. And I was resigned to being known as the wistful, slightly stupid space traveller home for a rest. I could even accept myself that way, and accept the many things I did not know and now could never learn.

Then one night, when we had forgotten to draw the curtain, I awoke and saw through the poplars a bright star shining. I sat awake and watched it until the movement of the planet had taken it past the window frame and from my sight. Lesser stars also wheeled by, but that one had been as bright as Sirius, my old beacon, the skywalker's dog star, and my heart was broken.

'You will go again,' said my friend.

'I will have to go,' I said, 'just as I planned. But I try to stop the time from arriving.'

'It will arrive,' said the alien. 'I always knew the stars would come for you.'

'Why did you come?' I said, made bold by despair and darkness. 'Did you come to judge us? Or to test us for merit? Why did you come among these trees and these tiny birds?'

'You feared that, and yet you brought me here?'

'I had little choice. I was asked to obey.'

'There's a paradox there, my friend.'

He had never before called me friend though I always addressed him so. I was not reassured but frightened by it.

'What have you found?' I said again, feeling there would be no answer.

'Pussy willows,' he said, and then laughed a bit in the darkness. He had learned to laugh near the start. He had needed a way to express ironies. 'I found pussy willows,' he repeated, and then paused before adding, 'worth the whole of the world.'

'Were they?' I said.

'On my home planet,' he said, 'there are no living trees, but there is a forest like this. It is made of glass, perhaps, or rock, or even illusion, and none can walk in it without going mad for at least a moment if not forever. That is because in a landscape that is only a shadow of life, one soon realizes that one is the only living thing, that death is all around and only you hold it from descending, and one cannot live with that knowledge. You have never lived on a dead world, but only in a dead ship with the memory of pussy willows to remind you of the earth around you. When I am out in space, I have nothing to remember.'

'And so you will remember pussy willows?'

'Nothing so simple as that. But it is a pleasant conceit.'

I turned on the light. Its cone of brightness closed the stars out as well as a curtain would have done. Looking at the now-black window in which I could see our reflections, distorted by the flow of the glass, I said, 'And what is the truth?'

He paused for a long time, watching me with that look of ambush, then said, 'Do you know, this is the first time you have questioned at all. Can it be you care?'

I made a sign with my hands. In reply, he smiled, shook his head and repeated, 'Do you care, for this world?'

'Of course I care,' I said. 'I call it home.'

'You break a branch to bring the little willow flowers home. What do you break when you take your memories out into space? When you were born your century had almost killed your planet. Now it is alive again, but you, have you changed?'

I pushed my hands away and out in a wide-fingered shrug. I don't know. How dare I know?

That's not enough, he said, for me or for anyone. I can't settle for that.

'Hence the difficulty of thinking and feeling,' I said.

'And if the fate of your world does indeed rest on me, what am I to decide from that? Is Terra worth saving for the Empire or the whole universe? Or is even your most cosmopolitan traveller a narrow-minded egotist light-years from understanding even self, let alone others?'

'Yes,' I said, 'that is certainly true, if you mean me. All the wisdom I lose every time I pass through the curtain is wisdom I must gain again, and if I choose to learn it from the creek and the trees and the beavers, what of it? I could choose less effective ways to learn. After all, they sent you here to find out the same thing – are we wise and can you find our wisdom? – and you have been skiing across deer trails, and playing the piano, and studying pussy willows, and you have perhaps arrived at some understanding. Of others, if not self.'

'You have the fallacy of the space traveller well into your bones,' he said. 'You think that you are the reason for everything. Because I was sent here with you, I am here to determine the fate of the world. Because you are here, this is where the judgment takes place. And you will tip the balance between life and death. You will save your home planet.' And he smiled at me with the fearful tenderness of a friend who loves one even when one is misguided.

It is hard to give up being the centre of the universe, but I do it when I fall to earth. But there is no guarantee that sometime I will not be wrong, and I told him that. He made no answer; instead, he reached for the switch on the bedside lamp. I held his hand from the panel. 'No,' I said, 'this must end somewhere.'

'We are all, in one way of speaking, human,' he said, 'and that is where it ends. Nothing more complicated. You seem to trust me despite yourself, and I am enjoying you also. That is all.'

Patiently, with his other hand, he lifted my hand from his and finished his motion to extinguish the light. He held my hand for a moment in the darkness. His fingers felt like leaves or twigs, I couldn't decide: brittle, dry, hard and cool. 'Don't worry,' he said, and I had to laugh. He laughed too and let go. I turned so that the stars could not find my eyes, pulled the covers around me, and went to sleep.

The next day I stayed on the main veranda most of the day, or walked near the lodge. Anna walked into the valley with my friend, and I saw them down by the willows. When I brought the scene close with my adjustable vision, I saw that they were looking at the branches very closely, their heads bent together to study each bud. The dense grey fur of the willow blossoms had given way to young leaves, and there was in my friend's face such a sadness that I was moved despite myself. They are gone, he said with his hands. Anna reached up and touched his face. They come again, I read her lips saying. I left them to themselves then. When they returned to the lodge at dinnertime, they both smiled at me with such an excess of good humour that I was almost sulky, and we were served dinner in a climate of silence. The stranger, the naturalist, came in a few minutes late, and the cook put a filled plate in front of her with an air of slight disapproval. She laughed as if at one of her obscure jokes, and looked at the three of us: Anna, my friend and me.

'So,' she said, 'you will both go back soon. Anna will have to return to her place in the city.'

Three silences for a moment, then I said, 'I don't think so.'

My friend smiled at me. 'You think you are seeing it now?'

I shook my head and made that common sign of baffled good humour. Everything is much simpler than it seems, I signed. Anna was the one who laughed. I looked at her. 'I am learning a new language myself,' she said.

'Languages!' said the naturalist, laughing too. 'Languages and natural history! It will all come to something after all, the great experiment!'

'I beg your pardon?' I said.

'I told you, the world will survive. I have made sure of it. I have found the evidence of regeneration. Of growth and change.'

'One only needed to come here in spring to find that. It has never been a secret to the local people,' said my friend.

'Ah, but evidence that would hold good off-planet,' she said, 'that's the problem. But I have prepared such a detailed study that they cannot possibly question the health of this biosphere. It has taken a very long time. And I have finished it here.' And from her pocket she took a record chip, the deep blue of governmental records, and showed it to us with a gleeful pride.

'That will save the world?' asked my friend slyly.

'That will provide the documentation. And for support . . . well, we can use your testimony if we have to, I suppose.'

'Use me where?' he said.

'Oh, at the hearing. If they think it important enough to have one. Sometimes they don't, just to grant continuance to a minor planet.'

'I'll come if you have the hearing on Terra,' he said. 'I won't be going away.'

'No,' said Anna, 'nor I to the city. I like the old language, and the new one.'

As for me, I was feeling my way through shock to understand just who the judge had been. 'How can you decide on such limited evidence?' I said.

'I don't decide. I just provide the evidence. Not limited evidence at all. You were hardly a factor.'

'I mean those lichens you showed me.'

'Oh, the lichen is very important,' she said. 'It is the canary in this particular coal mine. If the small, delicate organisms die, the large delicate organism that is the world will die, and we would need to get it out of the way then. And you, you could spread the death, we would have had to reconsider you. But it's all just a detail in a big frame.'

I looked to my alien friend: so I was after all just another tourist, even less important than you taught me to be – and who were you?

'I am just another organism on probation,' he said, 'but I have enjoyed my custody enough to stay once I am released. Like the Australians, I imagine, though I wouldn't like you to think I saw you as they saw the aboriginals in that land. If I am to stay here with Anna, I must have no such misunderstandings.'

'And are you to stay here with Anna?'

'Oh, yes, I think so,' Anna said, and my friend smiled.

'And for you,' said the stranger, looking at me, 'for you there are of course the stars, now that Terra will keep its membership in them. Will it be enough?'

'Almost,' I replied, 'and I imagine that the lichens and the aboriginals will welcome me when my next rest stop is due.'

'Oh, we'll take care of your forest for you, and have some people here to pamper you next time,' said Anna.

'As if you were the reason for it all,' said my friend, and all of us laughed, me most of all with relief, for there could have been no judgment better than the one I had heard. I had no wish to have been more influential in it. I had arrived, after all, at the end point of every visit, as just a small sample of the biosphere, a twig that can be snapped off and taken away, kept in development in an artificial medium, kept for a moment as a reminder of something that can never be sampled whole. And finally content to understand the relative importance of pussy willows, and the indulgent regard of those who love them.

So in due time I departed from my home and my friends, with private and public rituals of leave-taking, and with the tears I find come so easily to these new eyes of mine. I said all the goodbyes it was possible to say and I left them in early summer, with their happiness to hold them, and the promise of spring to come again each year. I went on to the work which in the end always claims me, the journeys and the new worlds. But still I visit there each time I am weary of star-gazing and want to rest for a while at home.

When I am there I stay in a holiday home made of logs. This story is of one visit I made, long ago. When next I was there, a tall friendly woman, with an attenuated beauty and arms so long her wrists gangled out of the old canvas coat was waiting to walk with me in the valley. She was the first of her kind to come into my world, but she took herself not at all seriously and had a sense of humour I enjoyed. She was very patient while I became strong, and she told me stories of my friend and Anna and what they had taught her, their daughter. Once, before I was fit enough to walk to the valley, she brought me a branch of the pink pussy willows, and handing it to me with a tentative gesture, said, 'My father would never cut them, but he said that I could do it for you, and that you would not abuse the privilege. I tried to do it the way he told me.' She knew the old language, and the sign language, and when I was too tired to talk, she would nest her hands into the signs for 'Don't worry,' and her laugh would echo across to the bluffs on the other side of the creek. But all this happened long afterward, in a different story, and many years ago. I only tell it to explain what finally came of my friend's simple visit. In the end the fate of the world as I had worried over it, as I had heard it summarized by someone who was basically only a government researcher, was incidental to the start of something else. Not the beginning of a whole new world, maybe, but at least the people of two worlds becoming one for the first time. But I had not a great deal to do with that either, and my stories are only the edges, the frame, for another, for every other story. Eventually I remember to be content with that.

On my home planet there are still poplar forests, with willow bushes growing beneath near the banks of small streams, and in the early spring before the snow is gone, the willows burst into soft bloom. If I am there at this time, and when I have reconciled with gravity, sometimes I walk down to gather pussy willows and memories. I still cut a branch, though now I feel a little guilty – but I learned my ways long ago, and my planet seems to continue in any case. At least, it is still alive, and so am I. In the end, the broken branches have been forgiven. That is the first thing I remember, and it gives me cause for much rejoicing.

Elisabeth Vonarburg
The Silent City

'Informed with a maturity of feeling too seldom
encountered in science fiction: a metamorphic journey into
disturbing possibilities of gender, social order, and genetic
science . . . '
William Gibson

While wild tribes roam the surface of the earth, the City,
deep underground, is the final storehouse of knowledge
and science. Only a handful of people survive there, kept
alive for multiple lifespans by machines. They are
conducting genetic experiments, and playing games of
deadly intent. Into this ghostly world of simulation and
dissimulation Elisa is born, and raised by her loving and
beloved father, Paul.

But as she grows up she begins to see the truth about the
City and her place in it. Rebelling against her father/lover,
she leaves the City for the outside world. Later, she will
return, having sown the seeds for a transformation of
human life.

The Silent City, by brilliant new Canadian writer Vonarburg,
engages with important issues of our time in a plot full of
twists and surprises.

Science Fiction   £4.95
ISBN: 0 7043 42189

Carol Emshwiller
The Start of the End of It All

'No-one writes like Carol Emshwiller. Absolutely no-one.
And no-one ever *has*. She is her own woman, has her own
voice, defies comparison, probes areas usually considered
dangerous, and is as close to being the pure artist as any
writer I have met.'
Harlan Ellison

When an alliance with alien invaders proves to offer as little
joy and comfort as relationships with human males, women
must take events into their own hands; in a strange
collection of ancient stones an old woman finds the dignity
and significance that society denies her; on a distant
icebound planet a hunter kills, and must face the
consequences of his action.

In this new collection of short stories Carol Emshwiller,
author of the successful *Carmen Dog*, shows us a world
changing at every moment. In the face of rigid systems of
belief and behaviour, her characters draw on inner strength
to transform themselves and the world around them. She
does not flinch from depicting human cruelty, but she also
celebrates the creativity of the human imagination and the
power of human love.

Science Fiction   £4.95
ISBN: 0 7043 4219 7